MASSACRE AND MARGINS

POE BAXTER BOOKS
BOOK 2

ACF BOOKENS

ACKNOWLEDGMENTS

With greatest thanks for the support of the Kickstarter campaign that will, as soon as possible, get these books into audio, I send my gratitude to Tiffany Ann, Sarah Davis, Jessica Bacho, Gladys Strickland, Jon Boisseau, Chris Adamson, Chris D'Antonio, and Stephanie C.

1

When my best friend Beattie changed our travel plans and surprised me with a trip to Iceland, I was nothing but thrilled. Well, except for the fact that I felt like I had nothing to wear. Beattie, however, assured me that our commissions from our first book acquisition for my uncle would cover a small shopping trip for beautiful wool coats and appropriate hats. That alone had me excited because while I was still coming into my own in terms of fashion, Beattie had long ago settled on her signature style and was all about helping me find mine. "You might find the perfect velvet blazer to go with that long black broomstick skirt you have," she said as we landed, planning our afternoon in the capital city's downtown.

But the long flight, the excitement of our last stop in Edinburgh, and the cold temperatures had me a little less than thrilled when we stepped off the plane in Reykjavik. Even with the promise of new clothes and the services of my favorite personal stylist, I just wanted to lie down and take a nap. Beattie was not to be deterred, though, and she insisted we check into our B&B and then get moving.

I did at least need a shower to wash the grime off my excitement. When we reached our lodgings, the aptly named Bed and Books, I smiled. The rooms were quaint, and I had visions of spending afternoons in the comfy reading chairs while immersing myself in Icelandic literature.

But first, my shower before we headed out to go shopping. Then, we had business to attend to. My uncle Fitz had sent us here on a book-buying mission for his rare bookshop in Charlottesville, Virginia, and while he had already set up a meeting with our contact about the title, I needed to do a little research to be sure I was prepared for the meeting.

Before I dug into my preparations, Beattie helped me purchase a bright yellow peacoat that I would never have even considered and convinced me that I really could pull off the plaid Doc Martens I'd wanted for twenty years. When we returned to our room, arms laden with unique and beautiful clothes, I felt rejuvenated enough to get to work.

I pulled out my laptop and searched for "Icelandic folklore." Very quickly, I found, not surprisingly, that many of the tales treasured in Scotland were also told here, if in a more Viking-like nature. Uncle Fitz's dossier on the book I was to acquire said it was a handwritten collection of elf stories, so I focused my research there.

I'd imagined creatures like Galadriel, shimmering elves with glowing skin and beatific countenances. Instead, the elves of Iceland were reclusive, smaller, and more cagey. Apparently, they had residences and, going by one report, even a church in the lava fields outside the city. When their territories were disturbed, though, they got vindictive and vengeful.

The more I read, the more I decided I liked the Icelandic elves far more than I liked Santa's or even Tolkien's. Those creatures had always seemed too good and wholesome for me. I appreciated an elf who got grumpy when someone tried to take her house.

According to Uncle Fitz's description of the book we'd come to acquire, the collection had been made in the twelfth century by a descendant of one of the original Viking families and was thus considered rare and valuable on two fronts: because of its early creation and because of its ties to some of the original settlers of Iceland. The collector who had asked him to obtain the book was, as he described himself to Uncle Fitz, of "old Viking blood" and wanted to add the book to his extensive collection of Viking material at his institution.

When the librarian had invited Fitz out to his estate west of Charlottesville, where his book collection was available to researchers, my uncle had gone because he was fascinated by both the old plantation house the man had restored and by the collection itself. Apparently, the man thought he might impress upon Uncle Fitz his seriousness by showing him the array of swords, helmets, clothing, and books he had amassed about, as he called them, his ancestors.

Little did this client know that my uncle took the requests of every client seriously, no matter their wealth, so such a show wasn't necessary. But from the video Uncle Fitz sent, with the client's permission, to show Beattie and me the collection as part of our background research, I knew my uncle had enjoyed every minute of that Greek Revival home, even if the Viking stuff wasn't really his cup of tea.

Uncle Fitz was a book collector, too, but his preference was for eighteenth- and nineteenth-century texts that dealt with slavery in the US. In fact, he had amassed one of the best collections of slave narratives around and regularly provided high-quality copies to scholars and genealogists. Upon his death, the collection was going to reside at the University of Virginia Special Collections Library. So when the video included a tour of the outbuildings and the existing slave cabin on the property, I wasn't surprised at all.

I watched Uncle Fitz's video again, trying to make out the

titles of the few dozen books I could see in a glass-front book-case. Most of them appeared to be histories, the sort of sagas that the Vikings were infamous for. But I could also see a couple more journal-like books similar to the one I was going to acquire.

As Fitz described it, the book was bound but not a formal book per se. It was more of a set of papers tied together between two pieces of sheepskin. The cover was a dark brown, and the paper—well, vellum, really—was yellowed with age. According to the few images Fitz had been able to acquire of the pages, most of the writing was faded, and some was nearly invisible. But according to Fitz's client, he had commissioned a well-known conservator to bring the book "back to its former glory."

Statements like that always made me nervous because the aging of a book was also part of its story, and the decision to make a book seem new was a dangerous one that could not only destroy the volume's value but also erase much of its own tale. But, as my uncle was quick to remind me, what our clients did with their books wasn't any of our business.

Next, I turned to the information Fitz had given me about our client, an older woman who lived in the Old West Side of Reykjavik. She had inherited the book from her mother, who had inherited it from hers, and so on. But the woman's grand-daughter, to whom she had planned to pass the book along as was the tradition, had decided she would rather the book be sold and her inheritance be in the form of money to use for her education.

I spent a few minutes lying on my bed and thinking about how the grandmother must feel. I imagine she was excited that her granddaughter had chosen education but also sad to see the book leave the family. I made a mental note to ask her about that when we met the next day to discuss the terms of the sale. I figured if she had told Fitz about that situation, she wouldn't mind me asking. And maybe it would help make the sale smooth if we were a little more emotionally connected.

After one last review of Fitz's notes, I closed up my laptop and looked over at Beattie, who was sound asleep on her bed. She acted the part of a seasoned traveler who had unlimited stamina but even the most well-traveled needed naps from time to time. And I was way less experienced in travel than she was, so I almost immediately joined my friend in a late-afternoon nap.

When I woke up, it was sometime between day and night, and I was afraid I had totally messed up my circadian rhythm by sleeping too long. I sat up and looked around, only to find Beattie just putting the finishing touches on her makeup. "Oh no, did I sleep all night?" I said as I bolted out of bed.

Beattie smiled. "Nope, it's only 7 p.m. Just in time for dinner." She grinned at me. "Although you might want to attend to those curls before we go out."

I walked over to the full-length mirror that hung beside the closet and squeaked. I looked like I had been electrocuted while I slept. My chin-length curls had gone from hanging down to standing out, and there was no taming these beasts at this point.

Instead, I decided to embrace the wildness and took out my trusty curtain tie-back that made the best hairband I'd ever found. Because of the texture, it never slipped in my hair, and it matched almost anything because it was off-white with bright-colored flowers on it. I put the band over my head, tied it at the nape of my neck, and then pulled it over my face so that all my curls were captured before sliding it back up and behind my ears. Then I slid a little curl cream through the wildest twists and called it good.

A few minutes later, dressed in my new peacoat and boots, I followed Beattie out the door and up the street to a restaurant that featured small tables and low lighting. "It's supposed to be the best cod in the city," she said.

"Oh joy," I said, ever the curmudgeon about seafood. "I guess I'll be having pasta."

Beattie took my arm. "Do you think I'd pick a place to eat for our first night in Reykjavik that required you to eat Italian? Give me more credit, Poe." She opened the door and told the hostess we had a reservation.

Then we followed the slim blonde woman to the back of the dining room and relaxed into our seats at a round table for two. The hostess slid two single-page menus in front of us and said she hoped we enjoyed our meal.

I scanned the options, expecting to find—despite my best friend's insistence to the contrary—that my only options were some sort of pasta dish or a mushroom thing. I loved mushrooms, but really, I can only eat mushrooms in so many ways. I was decidedly excited to see a variety of options I could try on the menu.

My food issues were odd and firmly entrenched, so lamb wasn't an option for me. I just couldn't get their bleating faces out of my head. Instead, I selected a cheese board that came with a variety of Icelandic cheeses, fresh rye bread, and slices of what our waiter told me was a classic Icelandic hot dog. Since I had long ago learned not to ask or think about what was in hot dogs, I followed that practice here.

After we ordered and Beattie had asked the waiter to bring us two truly Icelandic drinks, a request he maybe too-gleefully agreed to meet, we sat back and took a deep breath in unison. "It's beautiful here," I said. And it was. On the way in from the airport, I'd marveled at the mountains beyond the city, and when our taxi driver had turned into the city, I had loved the brightly colored houses that he told us were once the homes of sailors.

Here, in the downtown area, the buildings were different

and somehow made it feel like both a small town and an urban center. I could picture an American Hallmark movie being set here, but the streets also reminded me of the images I'd seen of places like Prague or Rome. But even with those associations, the city had its own vibe, something ancient but foreign to me. It was appealing in the way new but unthreatening places and people are. I loved it already.

When the waiter returned with our drinks, I smiled at the pink, frothy beverage he placed before me. "Crowberry cocktail" he said with a smile. "Icelandic vodka and our special berry liqueur." His accent was thick, but his English was perfect. "Enjoy slowly," he said with another grin.

The first sip I took knocked me back a little with its strength, but the following was sweet and just a little tart with a hint of vanilla. I quickly took another pull, but when I saw the waiter watching with a smile from the corner by the bar, I put the glass down and shot him a thumbs-up. It was delicious, but his caution about its strength seemed warranted. I could feel a warm bubble of delight in my stomach already.

And when the food came, I wasn't disappointed at all. The tray came with little signs, written in English, naming and describing each cheese, and no matter which one I placed on the small pieces of rye bread, I savored them all. The brie-like smooth cheese was my favorite, but I found, after I turned over the descriptive sign, that I also really liked the hot dog, which tasted more like mildly spiced sausage than American hot dogs.

By the time the waiter came back to ask about dessert, I was feeling full, but I'd seen a mention of ice cream with rhubarb syrup, and I couldn't pass it up. Beattie, ever the chocolate lover, chose the Chocolate Cake of Death, as the waiter described it, and when it arrived, it was the richest, densest chocolate cake I'd ever seen. We ended up sharing our desserts, which were both incredible, and after we paid the bill, we had to pry ourselves up because we were so full.

The walk back to the guesthouse was beautiful, with just a slight chill on the dark evening air, and when we got back to our room, I had a message from the bookseller that she was eager to meet tomorrow at 10 a.m., just as Fitz had arranged. It had been a good day all around, and I was exhausted.

But when I went to sleep, a tiny bit of foreboding crept in. I chalked it up to nerves and forced myself not just to ignore it but to think about cheese instead. My dreams that night were full of leaping sheep and crying cows.

THE NEXT MORNING I was up early, feeling refreshed and ready after a sound sleep in the very quiet room. It seemed like the city had taken a respite for a few hours because I was pretty sure even the road noise had died back while I slept. In any case, my animal-filled dreams hadn't disturbed me, and I was very eager to complete this purchase so Beattie and I could enjoy Iceland without the pressure of work over us.

The walk to the Old West Side address the seller had sent me was about twenty minutes, and given that the day was sunny and comfortable, Beattie and I donned our sweaters and best walking shoes and headed out around nine so that we could wander the streets on our way.

Despite the delicious breakfast, which had included skyr, a yogurt-cheese substance I'd considered smuggling back in my bag, and soft-boiled eggs for me, with the addition of fresh salmon for Beattie, we still stopped by a bakery and got something that looked like a giant Napoleon had a baby with a cream puff. We found a small bench and slowly but surely ate at least four people's worth of the goodness. I realized I was going to need a large bag for smuggling.

We stopped and window-shopped at a few little antique stores on the way, and while I could admire the beautiful objects, I knew they'd never hold the same draw for me as

American antiques did since I wasn't steeped in the genealogical roots and history of Iceland like I was at home. Still, I did see a tiny blue glass globe that I thought would be a perfect gift for Uncle Fitz, and I made a note on my phone to come back to the shop before we left for home.

When we arrived at our seller's house just before ten, I admired her beautiful cottage that sat right at the edge of the sidewalk with gables on four sides. The windows were six-paned and just wavy enough to look very old, and all the trim was painted a garden green that made a perfect contrast against the white siding and the bright blue sky above. It was the definition of quaint.

As soon as we knocked, a tiny blonde woman in a cardigan, jeans, and the pinkest sneakers I'd ever seen opened the door, and when she smiled, it felt like the whole world was going to be okay. "Ms. Jondanson?" I asked.

"Yes," she said. "You must be Ms. Baxter. Come in," she said before continuing with an apology for her excellent English.

"Well," I said after she gestured to a beautiful green settee by the front window of her small living room, "your English is far better than my Icelandic."

The woman laughed. "Coffee? Americans love coffee, I hear."

We both nodded. It was one of the most wonderful things we'd already learned about Iceland—these people loved coffee as much as we did. "Yes, please," Beattie said. "And if you have a bit of cream."

"Cream and sugar, of course," our new friend said.

As our host went to get our coffee, I looked around the room and admired the collection of tiny figurines in the corner. They reminded me of the Hummel figures my grandmother had collected, but these had what looked to be a Scandinavian influence, which made sense, of course.

When Ms. Jondanson came back with a tray filled with

cookies, coffee mugs, and the best-smelling coffee in the world, I smiled. "Thank you, ma'am. For the coffee and for meeting with us. We are honored."

The tiny woman waved a hand at us like we were preposterous with our gratitude. "Please," she said, "I am the one who is honored. I'm so grateful you're interested in our family's book."

Beattie smiled and said quietly, "If you don't mind us asking, are you okay with parting with it? It's been in your family for so long."

Ms. Jondanson nodded. "I am, but thank you for asking." She stared into the distance between the three of us for a moment and then continued. "I was disappointed at first, but then my granddaughter, who loves all things historical, convinced me that the book would be better with other people who could appreciate it, and she could do more good studying history than hoarding it."

My eyes teared up, and I swallowed hard to keep the tears from actually falling as I said, "That is beautiful."

"It is," Ms. Jondanson said. "It's really not my concern, I know, but do you have a buyer in mind?"

I shook my head. "Not as of yet, but for works like this, my uncle prefers to find public institutions as buyers. If he can manage, he also keeps the books in their country of origin." My uncle was firmly dedicated to communal wealth in the form of museums and libraries and far less committed to personal wealth, although the wealth of individuals was, as he reminded me, what kept his business operating. "I'm sure he's looking for a public buyer as we speak."

Ms. Jondanson smiled. "That's good news. I'll keep my eyes out for an announcement about its addition to a museum or such."

"Do you have any thoughts on where the book would be of

interest?" Beattie asked as she took a small notebook from her purse.

"Sögusafnið—er, I think you translate it the Saga Museum, comes to mind immediately," Ms. Jondanson said, "but that might be a little too casual for the book." She stood up and stared out the window as if the cityscape might help her think. "But maybe Safnahúsið, the Culture House, might be better. It's a more solemn place, more fitting for an old book of stories."

Beattie made notes, and I watched her pause as she tried to spell the Icelandic words. We'd have to look up the spellings later. "Thank you," she said. "I'll let Fitz know."

"It would be lovely to visit the book and if it stayed here in Reykjavik, where it has always been." Ms. Jondanson sat back down and offered us a refill of our coffee, which we gladly took.

"Has your family been in the capital from the beginning of Norse settlement?" I asked, stumbling a bit as I tried to figure out the best way to ask the question without erasing the indigenous history here or offending our host.

She nodded. "We were some of the original Vikings," she said. "But there were no indigenous people here," she said. "We plundered and pillaged a lot of places, but Iceland was ours to take." She smiled. "Well, sort of. The Irish were here first, but most people don't think of the monks as settlers."

I laughed. I appreciated someone who could take a poke at their heritage, especially since so many of my fellow Americans were so serious about things like the Revolutionary War and so flippant about the slaughter of our indigenous populations. Plus, I was curious about why there hadn't been indigenous people here . . . just too darn far north for most, I imagined.

"So you're a founding family," Beattie said with a bit of awe in her voice. "That's commendable."

"Well, we didn't sail over ourselves," she said, "but we are proud of our ancestors." She stood again. "Would you like to see the book?"

Beattie and I both broke into wide grins. "Yes, please!" I fairly bounced in my seat while Ms. Jondanson stepped to a small desk in the corner of the room and brought out a leather-bound book that looked far more like a journal I might have made at summer camp in sixth grade than it did one of the greatest works of Icelandic folklore.

I glanced over at Beattie, who was vibrating with excitement, too, but she knew this sort of book was my passion. So she let me reach out and take the book carefully from Ms. Jondanson's hands.

It was exquisite in its simplicity. The measurements were about six inches by eight inches, smaller than most older books. I presumed that was because it had been made with hand tools rather than any sort of mechanized press. The covers were thick leather and a deep, dark gray. I ran my fingers over the smooth surface and realized, without knowing quite how, that it wasn't cow's leather like I was used to.

"Seal skin," Ms. Jondanson answered in response to my silent question. "Frowned upon today, for sure, but back then, seals provided everything. And their hides are tough, far tougher than those big wet eyes might lead you to believe." A twinkle spun through her eyes as she spoke.

"Wow," I said as I caressed the cover one more time before opening the first page carefully. The next page was covered from top to bottom and left to right in handwriting as if the author knew that the vellum was rare and wanted to fill every bit. The ink had browned to a dark color, but parts of it were so light that I could barely see them. Of course, I couldn't read modern Icelandic, much less medieval Norse, so I had no idea what it said. We had a meeting later today with scholars to provide us with a translation of at least the first few pages so that we could use those as we sought a buyer.

"Your ancestor wrote this," Beattie said as she ran one finger over the page.

"She did," Ms. Jondanson said. "She was a rare woman."

"Even in a country that elected the first female president in the world?" Beattie asked.

"Even so," the older woman said. "We fought hard for her, and I'm almost as proud of her as I am of my female ancestors who kept this book."

I wanted to clutch the book to my chest, and I could tell even the stoic Beattie was getting a bit emotional. A book written by a woman and then preserved by her women descendants—what a treasure. We didn't get to hear about—let alone see and touch—such treasures often. "Thank you for trusting us with this precious heirloom," I said with a little crack in my voice.

"Meeting the two of you and seeing that two women are being entrusted with the care of one part of my family's legacy has made me even more confident in our decision to sell the book." She cleared her throat. "Now, not to be crass, but how do we do the business?"

I smiled. "It's just a matter of discussing payment and signing some paperwork. Then we give you a check, and you give us the book." I looked carefully at Ms. Jondanson. "We can always come back tomorrow if you'd like more time."

The woman shook her head. "No, I feel sure, and to be honest, sometimes it's best to rip the bandage off quickly."

I knew that feeling all too well. "Very good," I said. "I believe you and my uncle discussed a price."

From there, the sale went without incident, and thirty minutes later, Beattie and I walked out of her house with the book, promising that we'd keep her informed about its placement as soon as we could.

2

The walk back to our room was quiet. I felt the weight of the history we carried with us now, and I expected Beattie did too. When we were safely behind closed doors, we slipped the book into the fake dictionary we'd picked up during our last trip to Edinburgh and locked it up tight. We'd decided we'd carry it with us everywhere, given the trouble we'd had on our last buying excursion. It wasn't ideal, given the weight of the book safe and the book, but hopefully, we wouldn't be hauling around a unique historical artifact for long.

We had just enough time to grab a snack before we met with the language scholars, so we headed to a bubble tea place just up the road from the museum where we were to meet. Our hometown, Charlottesville, was just moving, finally, into the bubble tea craze, and I was missing my lavender tea. Fortunately, Cha Time was a wonderful café, and both of us got huge bubble teas to go.

As we wandered down the street, I enjoyed the contrast of this rather contemporary Taiwanese drink with the quaint European buildings around us. I was quickly learning that one of the great things about international traveling was that you could go deep into the culture of the place you were visiting *and* also enjoy some of the world's best delights, like tapioca balls in milk tea. Globalization certainly had its drawbacks, but it also had its delights.

The museum where our contacts, Inga Sigurðardóttir and Gunnar Annasson, were going to meet us was a few blocks away, so we enjoyed our mid-day stroll through the downtown area. Many of the buildings were big, like those in major American cities, but they also reminded me of small towns I'd visited in the Hudson River Valley of New York or even the ski towns of Colorado. There was just something quaint and accessible about the stores we passed and the gentle kindness of the residents' faces.

And the museum itself was a treat in many ways, including the fact that it the Saga Museum that Ms. Jondanson had recommended. We hadn't made the connection because, well, our Icelandic was terrible, but as soon as we were welcomed by the docent in English, we smiled at each other. Once again, the twists of our experience were bringing us to just the right place.

The building reminded me of an old American high school building with a flair of something maybe Danish. It was far more beautiful than most high schools in the States, with its intricate brickwork and ornate windows, but the symmetrical layout and block construction of the building made me think of the old schools that were being turned into community centers and art galleries back home. I loved it immediately for that reason.

Inside, the central stairwell was marble and far more utilitarian than I had expected, but as soon as we turned into the first exhibit room, where the guide told us we'd meet our contacts, I gasped. The room was dark, with soft yellow lights shining down on some of the oldest books I had ever seen. As I moved slowly to the nearest tome, the guide explained that this was an exhibit of Norse sagas that described the founding of Iceland in the ninth century.

The book before me was handwritten, much like the one secured in my tote bag. A portion of the text had been translated into both Icelandic and English, and as I read the translation, I was swept up in the great story of sea travel and storms. I had never been someone inclined to great adventure except on the page, but these words made me long for the days when travel wasn't quite as easy as boarding a plane.

That travel had often been as deadly as it was successful, so I realized I was being far too romantic in my thoughts about Norse history, especially given the plundering and pillaging Ms. Jondanson had mentioned earlier. But I couldn't help myself. I was swept up in the moment.

My attention was pulled away from the books, however, when I felt a warm hand on my arm and turned to see a familiar face beside me. "Adaire Anderson, what are you doing here?" I said a bit too loudly and then listened as my voice echoed around the room. I could feel myself blushing as I looked at him.

He blushed, too, and then said, far more quietly, "Your uncle was kind enough to tell me you had come to Iceland on the hunt for his next acquisition, and we thought we might come over and surprise you."

"We?" I said just as my eyes found the locked lips of Beattie and Adaire's brother Aaran. "Oh, you both came."

Adaire leaned over and kissed my cheek. "Is that okay?" he asked, and I could see the nervousness in the small lines around his eyes.

"Of course, it's okay. What do you know about Norse sagas?" I said with a laugh.

"Quite a bit, actually," another man's voice said behind me. "Adaire, it's good to see you."

I looked from the tall, blond man who had stepped forward

to shake Adaire's hand to the face of the man I had been on two dates with back in Edinburgh and just stared.

The blond man caught my gaze and put his hand out to me. "Gunnar Annasson. You must be Poe Baxter?" His accent was definitively Icelandic, but I detected a bit of a roll in his Rs that sounded familiar.

"Nice to meet you," I said as I shook his hand. "You and Adaire know each other, I presume?"

"Went to University together," Annasson said. "The world of books is small, as I imagine you know, Ms. Baxter."

Just then, Beattie and Aaran joined us, as did a dark-haired woman with the whitest skin I had ever seen. She looked like a doll, she was so fine-featured, and when I shook her hand, I had to fight the impulse to be overly gentle lest I break her bones.

"Inga Sigurðardóttir," she said as she applied more than the necessary amount of pressure to my hand. I wondered if she had to compensate for her diminutive stature with brute force and tried to be casual as I stretched my fingers to relieve the bit of pain she had caused.

"Nice to meet you," Beattie said as she introduced herself and Aaran to the group. Then, introductions all made, Inga—I was already beginning to call her Inga in my head because I had no confidence in my ability to pronounce her last name correctly—led us down a small hallway to a meeting room with a circular table and beautiful landscape paintings on the wall.

There, we found a carafe of coffee and some more of those pastries that Beattie and I had wolfed down the day before, but this time, they were cut into more personally-sized pieces. I was glad I wasn't being introduced to them for the first time today because I knew I wouldn't have been able to be polite and eat only one piece if I hadn't prepared mentally.

Now, though, my belly full of bubble tea and my mind completely aware of where I could get—what I learned just then—Vínarbrauð, I was able to pass on the pastry and instead help myself to a cup of delicious, perfectly hot coffee.

As we sat down, Adaire held out my chair, and I blushed again. He just smiled at me and then took a seat to my left. Beattie sat on my other side with Aaran next to her, and then Gunnar and Inga.

Never one to start a conversation smoothly or with any form of decorum, I said, "Please, everyone, call me Poe. And if you don't mind, I'll call you Inga and Gunnar because I really don't want to mispronounce your beautiful last names with my horrible Icelandic."

"Poe, it is," Gunnar said with a smile.

Inga, however, glowered at me. But she didn't say anything, and I took that as acquiescence to my very American and very limited facility with languages. "Thank you," I replied. "We're so excited to be here."

As I spoke, Beattie reached into her bag and pulled out the third member of our traveling party, Butterball, the hamster, and set him on the table in his transparent plastic carry bag. Inside the bag, he had a tiny toy shaped like sushi, and he had his head propped on it like a pillow.

In an instant, Inga was up and cooing over the little rodent. She talked to him in the sweetest voice, and somehow, I knew she was telling him how handsome he was, even though she was speaking Icelandic. BB, for his part, simply lay there, pretending to be asleep—I had seen him peek as Beattie lifted him from the bag—and letting himself be admired. He was probably scheming about how he could get a pastry or perhaps climb into the sugar bowl.

Not everyone was as keen on the pet Beattie and I shared as Inga was. We had learned, for example, that Americans did not like his presence in restaurants, a fact at which he took great offense, and my dentist had made it very clear that I was not to bring BB back for my next cleaning, no matter how much her hygienist begged me to do so.

Inga, however, asked if she could hold him, and although Beattie suggested she keep him in the bag, she let the historian carry the bag to her side of the table, where she gave the little guy some of the best pets of his life. I wondered if BB would like to move to Iceland because he sure seemed to be enjoying himself.

As Inga continued to love on our hamster, Gunnar said, "Thank you for inviting us to consult with you about the book you have acquired. It is, indeed, an honor."

Beattie smiled. "No, we are thrilled to meet with you. Thank you."

I grinned. "Yes, thank you. It's hard for us to evaluate the worth of a book we cannot even read." I reached into my bag and took out the dictionary safe, setting it on the table, and then discreetly entered the combination on the front.

When I pulled out the volume, gasps passed around the table, and while I wanted to hand the book to Adaire first—out of some sort of loyalty, I supposed—I passed it to Gunnar. He held the book gently and opened a few pages, his mouth slightly open the whole time.

After he and Inga had both looked at the book casually, they asked permission to do a more formal investigation. "To determine the date," he said.

I looked over at Beattie to be sure she didn't have a hesitation, and when she nodded, I said, "Sure. We do not want to damage the book, but we do need to authenticate it, of course."

Inga nodded and then carefully trimmed a minuscule piece off one of the middle pages before dropping it into a test tube. "We'll take this back to our lab and analyze it for you. It will take one to two days."

I nodded. "Thank you." I watched them study the vellum with their magnifying glasses. They peered closely at each page, and each of them made notes in separate notebooks. About fifteen minutes after they began, they switched notebooks and compared.

"We believe, based on our visual examination, that the book is authentic, but the analysis will be largely definitive," Inga said. "If it is authentic, we would be interested in making the purchase as soon as possible."

"Oh," I said. "You want to buy it?" I glanced over at Beattie, who looked just as surprised as I was. "I wasn't aware."

Gunnar nodded. "We prefer to see items before we make the interest of the government known."

"The government?" Beattie said. "The Icelandic government wants to buy the book."

"If it is what we all believe it to be," Adaire said, "it is a national treasure. I suspect you'd display it at the national museum."

"Yes," Inga said. "You saw the other books of sagas as you came in?"

We all nodded. "This would be another item for that collection." She met my gaze and held it. "The president would like to ask you a personal favor."

I cleared my throat. "The president? Of the country?"

A small smile crept onto her lips. "Yes. He asks that you not look for other buyers until we have had the, what do you call it, the right of first refusal. Is that acceptable?"

This time I didn't have to get confirmation from Beattie. It was always Uncle Fitz's desire to keep books in their place of origin. Plus, if the president of a country asked for something, it seemed wise to comply if at all possible. "Of course," I said.

"We also need to ask that you please not tell anyone about the book beyond those who must know," Beattie said. "You can imagine how difficult the conversation might be for us if people inquired and we were not at liberty to discuss the book's current status."

Inga and Gunnar nodded. "Agreed. We will be in touch as soon as we have our results," she said. "I trust you will come with purchase figures in mind."

I nodded again. "Of course." Apparently, this was the only phrase I could pull forth from the word vaults of my shocked brain. I slid my card across the table to our new colleagues, and Beattie did the same.

"Now, please enjoy the rest of the Culture House. We have arranged to have a private tour for the four of you," Gunnar said as he stood. "We will be in touch."

For a few moments after they left, I just sat there, staring at the book in my hands. If that alone wasn't wonderful enough, I was now, apparently, just one degree of separation from the president of Iceland. "That just happened, right?" I said quietly.

Beattie took the book out of my hands and tucked it back into its dictionary safe. "Yes, Poe. That just happened."

"You really didn't know who you were meeting when you came, did you?" Adaire said.

"You did?" I asked as I stared at him.

"Inga and Gunnar are the heads of the collections department of the national library here. They work directly for the president himself." Adaire smiled. "Maybe I should have mentioned that?"

I shook my head. "Maybe?" I stowed the fake dictionary back in my bag and gently picked up Butterball's bag, noting that he was, again, sound asleep. It must be nice not to be fazed by momentous things or any things, really.

The next two hours were delightful as the four of us wandered the collections in the Culture House with our personal guide. She gave us the history of the building and how it had been the original national museum but was now used more for exhibitions, community meetings, and performances. As we finished the tour, she said, "The president has provided four tickets for tonight's private concert with Björk if you'd like to attend."

I nearly dropped my bag and came close to collapsing on the floor. "We are invited to a private concert with Björk," I whispered.

Fortunately, Beattie maintained her sanity and took the tickets from the woman's hand. "Thank you very much. Please thank Mr. President for us as well." She paused as if considering something. "Will he be in attendance tonight? I only ask because I want to be sure to follow proper protocol."

I had no idea what the proper protocol for meeting a president was, but I was pretty sure it involved a new outfit and a massive pep talk for my brain so that I wouldn't look like I had the vocabulary of a two-year-old.

"He will not be here this evening, so no need to worry," she said before thanking us for taking time at the Culture House and walking with us to the front door.

As we walked down the street back toward our rooms, I was torn between wanting to spend a little bit of time with Adaire and feeling the need, even though the president wouldn't be there, to buy a special outfit for tonight. Fortunately, Beattie made the decision for me when she asked the men, "Did you happen to bring suits?"

Aaran and Adaire looked at each other, and Adaire said, "Why no, we didn't. Looks like we all need to go shopping."

Aaran grumbled, "Really, a suit?"

"I'll help you pick one out, handsome. You're going to look great," Beattie said as she tucked her arm into Aaran's. "Meet at the guesthouse in two hours."

I glanced down at my watch. "Will that give us time for dinner?"

"Definitely," Beattie said as she peeked at the tickets she'd tucked into her bag. "The concert isn't until eight."

"But the guys need to go change." I turned to Adaire. "Does that give you enough time?"

"Well, we're staying where you are, so if it's enough time for you, I suppose it will be enough for us." He winked at me.

"You knew they were coming?" I said as I turned to my best friend.

"I may have gotten a text from Aaran yesterday," she said with a smirk. "I wanted to surprise you."

"Actually," Adaire said as he took my hand. "I asked her not to tell you. You said you love surprises."

I grinned. I did love surprises. "Okay, see you all in two hours," I said as I pulled Adaire up the street and into a small alley, where I gave him the welcome kiss he deserved.

"That was a nice surprise," he said.

"I take it you like surprises, too," I said with my own wink. "Help me pick a dress?" I tugged him back onto the street and toward a boutique I'd seen the day before when we were buying more utilitarian clothes.

"Of course. What color are we looking for?" he asked as we stepped inside a veritable rainbow of fabric. "Might I suggest a teal?" He pulled out the skirt of a chiffon, empire-waisted dress that would flatter my figure well.

"I'll definitely try it out," I said as I lifted a red cocktail dress from another rack.

We made our way around the shop, and when it was time for me to go to the dressing room, he followed me back "to help." As I tried on the first dress, I wondered how Beattie was faring. Given that she was quite tall, finding clothes could sometimes be hard . . . and then I wondered if Aaran had volunteered to help her as Adaire had me. Suddenly, I had a pressing question.

"Adaire, how does your brother feel about Beattie?" I asked.

He looked at me in surprise, but then I supposed he saw the concern on my face and sobered a bit. "He really cares about her," he said.

I stepped out of the dressing room in the red cocktail dress and turned so Adaire could zip the back. "That's good." I stood in front of the mirror and looked at myself before turning to face Adaire.

Adaire's face changed as he put the pieces together for my question and my concern. "Aaran knows she is trans. She told him a while back. He told me he doesn't care about what's under her clothes if that's what you're worried about. He just cares about her."

A wave of relief washed over me. "Okay, good. We hadn't really talked about it, she and I, and then when you showed up today . . ."

"Right, that part of the surprise probably wasn't ideal," he pulled me into a quick hug. "But you don't have to worry. I don't know the details, but Aaran made sure I knew he knew and that he didn't care."

I smiled. "Excellent. Now, let's talk about this dress. I do care, and I don't like it."

"You look beautiful," he said, "but I don't think this is the one."

I smiled and went back into the dressing room. I tried on everything I'd picked out, and none of them were right. But when I slipped into the teal chiffon Adaire had picked, I knew immediately just by the feel that the dress was perfect.

And Adaire's expression when I stepped out confirmed it. His eyes got wide, and a flush spread up his cheeks. "Wow," he said, "Oh, Poe, this one is bonnie." His brogue got a little deeper as he spoke.

I looked down with embarrassment, but when I finally turned and caught a glimpse of myself in the mirror, I couldn't disagree. The dress hung lightly against my hips, and it made my collarbone look like Kiera Knightley's. It was the perfect blend of Jane Austen meets Met Gala, and I loved it. "This is the one," I said and felt—almost—like those brides on that show where they pick their wedding gowns.

As soon as that thought crossed my mind, though, I forced it out. This wasn't a wedding gown, and Adaire and I weren't even really dating. I was getting way ahead of myself—no, not just ahead of myself, into a new lane that hadn't even been marked yet. I took a long, deep breath.

"It is the one," Adaire said as he stepped so close behind me that I could feel his breath on my neck. "You are beautiful." He placed a soft kiss on my neck, and my breath caught.

No lane yet, Poe. No lane, I thought. "I'm going to get it," I said as I stepped forward and away from him before I lost myself completely.

"No, I am," he said as he carefully removed the safety-pinned tag and headed to the counter.

I stared after him, not sure what to do since I was in a gorgeous gown that I had been planning to charge and pay off over, say, the next five years. But then I heard Beattie's voice in my head, "Take the gift, Poe. Let him have this."

I took a deep breath, went back into the dressing room, and decided I needed to make my own lane, starting tonight.

FORTUNATELY, Adaire was a decisive man, and he was able to quickly pick a charcoal-gray suit with a thin cream stripe, a lovely cream shirt, and a gorgeous paisley tie with just a bit of the same teal color as my dress. Then we hustled back to our rooms to get changed.

When I burst in, I almost ran right into Beattie, who was standing in front of the mirror in a long, satin sheath that fit her perfectly. The simple lines of silver cloth accentuated her height but in a way that highlighted her willowy figure and graceful movements. She'd found some silver ballet flats, which seemed wise because she and Aaran were matched in height if she didn't wear heels. Her hair was swept up in a chignon. She looked just a bit edgy and altogether gorgeous.

Without a word, I stripped and then stepped into my dress, and when Beattie turned to look at me, she gasped. "Poe, that dress is perfect."

"Adaire picked it," I said and blushed. "Actually, he bought it for me."

"Those Anderson men. Aaran bought these for me," she pointed to a graceful chain-link necklace and matching earrings that were so perfectly my best friend's style that I could have cried. They were six parts rock 'n' roll and four parts elegance, just like her.

"Okay, now you need shoes," Beattie said. "These will be perfect." She tugged a pair of silver pumps out of my bag. "But they need something." Then from out of her "bag of magic," as I called the small clutch she kept with beauty odds and ends, she tugged two silver ribbons. "Put your legs up on the bed."

I had long ago learned not to challenge my friend and smoothed my dress below me as I followed her direction. She wrapped the ribbons around my ankles and tucked the ends into the backs of my shoes. "There," she said. "Now, your makeup and hair."

Ten minutes later, my hair was held back by a thin circlet of silver that Beattie had acquired for me while she shopped, and my makeup was shimmering and romantic. In contrast to her dark eyeliner and bright lips, I looked demure, which I actually liked for the night. I felt not only demure but beautiful, and for once, I was okay with playing that up.

When the men met us in the foyer of the guesthouse, both of them whistled, and I stopped dead on the steps when I saw Adaire in his suit. His dark curls were styled with something that made them more noticeable, and he'd left a carefully groomed line of shadow on his jaw. The tie brought out the flecks of gold in his eyes, and when I finally forced myself to move over and hug him, I breathed in the rich scent of a cologne that felt both nautical and woodsy. He was so swoon-worthy that I could hardly stand it.

Our host had recommended a little restaurant around the corner to the men, so we walked that way after donning cloaks she let us borrow. When we entered, I sighed. The whole place was lit by candlelight, and we were taken to a small table for four by the front window that looked out on the quiet street. This night just kept getting more and more perfect.

Our food was delicious, but I couldn't tell you much about it because I was so distracted by Adaire and the fact that he kept his ankle pressed against mine for the entire meal. Between that bit of flirting and the very good Icelandic wine we had, I was giddy by the time we stood to leave for the concert, and I took Adaire's arm, both to be close to him and to steady myself.

The concert hall was a beautiful room that was hung completely in deep blue velvet drapes, and the room was small, with perhaps seating for twenty. Our seats were up front, in the second row, and beside us sat Inga and Gunnar, holding hands. "You two are a couple," I said before I could stop myself.

Inga smiled. "We are. It's good to see you again," she said as I sat down next to her. "And you two are a couple as well, I see?" She looked at where I had set my hand on Adaire's knee without thinking.

I blushed and nodded, not sure what to say.

"We are," Adaire answered as he leaned over me, then Inga to shake Gunnar's hand.

I caught his eye, and he winked before leaning close to me. "If that's okay with you," he said.

"Of course," I said and kissed his cheek. "But we may need to talk logistics."

"I have a plan," he said and put his hand over mine on his leg. "Don't you worry, lass."

Oh, I wasn't worrying. I was very busy swooning.

The music was gorgeous, and Björk was stunning in her simple dress and tall boots. I didn't know her music well, but it left me feeling haunted in the best way, as if I'd just spent the evening with fairies and elves and was carrying the aura of their magic with me.

The whole night was spectacularly beautiful, and when Inga and Gunnar invited us to meet Björk after the show, we couldn't resist. I didn't want the night to end. And while I was a bit too shy to actually say anything to the superstar singer, I did shake her hand and listened as she and Beattie discussed a group called Iona that they both loved.

As the seven of us talked, I noticed a stocky, long-haired woman with a sallow complexion waiting by the door. She was bouncing from foot to foot, and I wondered if she had to go to the bathroom or was waiting to say hi to Björk herself.

When we thanked the singer for her performance one last time and headed for the door, the woman who had been lingering stepped in front of me. "Poe Baxter," she said. "I'm Erika Weber, and I'd like to talk to you about the collection of sagas you are selling."

Out of the corner of my eye, I saw Inga and Gunnar pass a look between them, and I felt my guard go up just a bit. "Nice to meet you, Ms. Weber. But I'm afraid you're mistaken." I didn't want to lie to the woman, so I didn't say anything further. The book was not currently for sale after all.

She tilted her head and smiled at me in a way that made me want to scrub my skin with a hard-bristled brush. "We both know that is not true."

I felt Adaire take my arm, and on my other side, Beattie stepped forward. But their gestures were acts of solidarity, not actions of distrust in my ability to handle the situation. "Ms.

Weber, we have just met, and you have already accused me of lying. I wish you a good evening, but I am going now." I moved to step around the woman, who blocked most of the doorway, but she stepped into my path.

"I'm afraid I must insist, Ms. Baxter." She smiled again, and this time, her look made my teeth hurt.

Aaran stepped forward and physically moved the woman aside. From my perspective, it looked like he had to put a considerable amount of his fisherman's muscle into his actions, but she did move over a couple of feet. Then Aaran turned his body sideways and motioned for us to walk by.

Once we were past her, Ms. Weber followed us down the stairs into the foyer. "I don't think we understand each other," she said. "My employer must have that manuscript, and he would like it this evening."

At that moment, I finally registered her accent. It was the phrase *this evening* that made the association for me because it called up an image of Dracula. *She must be Romanian*, I thought. "That is not going to happen," I said with as much finality as I could. "If your employer wishes to discuss books, he can call Fitzhugh Simmons at Demetrius Books in the States. Good night."

I turned to go and felt everyone else turn as well, but then Beattie yelped beside me and said, "What in the world?"

"Let her go," Aaran shouted.

Ms. Weber had Beattie by the arm and was pulling her back into the foyer. "As I've said, we will complete this transaction this evening."

Just then, a large man in a black suit came down the stairs, took Ms. Weber by the arms, and pulled her backward. "Björk wishes you a good evening," he said as he continued to drag the woman away.

If the whole situation hadn't been very scary, I might have laughed at the sight of Ms. Weber trying to fight against a man who was almost double her size. Somehow, though, I didn't think this would be the last we saw of her, and instead of laughing, I collapsed against Adaire once we were outside.

"Perhaps," Inga said, "you will allow us to call you a taxi. The walk to your lodgings is not advisable, it seems."

Adaire nodded. "Thank you. We will wait there"—he pointed to a coffee shop on the corner—"for the ride."

"Most recent events aside," Gunnar said, "I hope you enjoyed your evening."

All of us nodded, and I said, "It was lovely. Please thank the president for us." I wasn't sure that was something appropriate or fitting to say, but I meant it. The whole night had felt like an honor.

Gunnar and Inga waved as they walked up the street, and Gunnar put his phone to his ear to call us a cab. The four of us checked traffic and then jogged across the street and sat in the back of the coffee shop while we waited for our ride.

3

The magical mood from the concert still lingered with me, but on top of it, I felt a growing sensation of dread. I wasn't afraid exactly, but I did think we were in the middle of something far less simple than it had seemed just a few hours before.

I had wanted to ask Inga and Gunnar if they knew Ms. Weber, but I hadn't wanted to stall in the middle of the sidewalk while we talked. I figured I'd reach out to them in the morning to ask. Besides, despite the fact that I really liked them, someone had leaked the information about the book, and it could have been them.

As if she were reading my thoughts, which maybe she was, Beattie said, "So, do we think our government compadres spilled the beans?"

I shook my head. "I have no idea, but I don't think so. That does beg the question of who did, though. It wasn't any of us, I'm sure." I was *almost* sure, but when I saw the looks on my friends' faces, I became certain. They were mortified at even the suggestion they would have breached this confidence.

"I've been thinking about that," Adaire said. "Did you discuss confidentiality with the seller?"

Beattie and I caught each other's eyes and then shook our heads. "It didn't even occur to me," she said. "It was her book, after all."

"Same," I said. "And honestly, we didn't know it mattered then. It wasn't until we met Inga and Gunnar that they asked us to keep the sale quiet."

"True," Adaire said. "Do you think she might have told someone?"

I shrugged. "I don't know, but she might have. If I'd come into a sizable paycheck, I might have let someone know."

"Like her granddaughter," Beattie said firmly. "I bet she told her granddaughter."

The accuracy of that surmise felt like a lightning bolt in my mind. "Oh, I'm sure she did, which means we need to talk to that granddaughter."

Beattie nodded, so did Adaire, but Aaran looked quizzical. "Why is that exactly?" he asked.

"Because we need to know who she told and figure out who sent Ms. Weber after us," Beattie said.

"And why is that?" Aaran countered.

"Because she threatened us," Beattie replied, her voice getting a little harsh.

I put a soft hand on my best friend's arm. "For that reason, yes, but also because we need to understand the circumstances around the book. If it's that much in demand, that could affect the price." I wasn't sure why Beattie was quite so upset that she'd lost track of the professional side of this situation, but I did know she wouldn't want me asking about that in front of the men.

Aaran nodded. "Because that means it might be worth more than you thought," he said as he wrapped an arm around Beattie.

"Precisely," Adaire said. "Competition always drives up the price. If it works for fish, it works for books." He grinned at his brother.

"Well, except for the filleting part. That doesn't work so well for books," I said with a smile, hoping to lift Beattie's mood a little, but she didn't even so much as blink. Something was really bothering her.

OUR TAXI ARRIVED A MOMENT LATER, and Beattie, Aaran, and I got into the back seat while Adaire sat next to the driver and gave him the address. Soon, we were back in the house, where our host had set out cookies and coffee next to a bottle of whiskey. On most nights, that would have been really appealing, especially given how cold it was outside. But tonight, I just wanted to be alone with Beattie and figure out what was going on.

The guys sat down to enjoy a drink of whiskey sans the coffee, but Beattie and I decided to call it a night. I told Adaire I'd text him with our plans for the morning. He nodded quietly, and I knew he understood my friend needed me.

We climbed the red-carpeted stairs to our room in silence, and I didn't push Beattie when we got inside and undressed. It wasn't until we'd settled in our beds that I said, "Are you okay?"

She groaned and slid further under the down comforter. "I don't know," she said from beneath the blanket. "That whole situation freaked me out."

"It was definitely scary. What freaked you out the most?" I asked.

The top of her head and eyes appeared over the covers. "You promise not to laugh?"

"Beattie, when have I ever laughed at you," I said. "Okay, besides that time you tried to wear Hammer pants in eighth grade."

This made her smile, and she sat up altogether. "I really thought I could pull them off," she said.

"You couldn't, but moving on," I said with a laugh. "Seriously, what is it?"

She stared at me for a moment and then looked down. "That woman. She scared me."

I wasn't inclined to laugh, but I did feel shocked. I had never known Beattie to be scared of anyone, especially not a bully of a woman who was more than a foot shorter than her. "She did? What about her scared you?"

Beattie shook her head. "It's probably nothing."

"If it scared you, Beats, it's not nothing." I got up and went to sit on her bed. "Tell me."

She sighed. "I honestly thought she was going to hurt me."

"Like shoot you or something?" I said, my concern growing deeper.

"Worse. I think she had a knife." She curled up into a ball beneath the blankets. "I don't really know why I think that. I didn't see one, but I thought she might cut me."

I shuddered. "Then we definitely need to go to the police in the morning," I said. "We probably should have gone tonight, but I didn't realize how serious this situation was."

"I could just be imagining the whole thing," Beattie said quietly.

"You, my friend, are not one prone to fits of imagination. If you felt threatened, then you were threatened. All of us saw her grab you. We have a case for assault, and at the very least, we can ask the police to keep an eye out for her. Maybe that'll discourage her from bothering us again." I didn't believe that for a moment, but I wanted to believe it for Beattie's sake. I really did.

"Thanks, Poe-Poe," she said as her head fell to her pillow. "I'm going to go to sleep now."

"Want me to sleep with you?" I said.

She lifted the covers, and I slid in beside her. "It's like high school all over again." Beattie's high school years had been really brutal, and many a night, she'd stayed at my house in my bed because she felt safe there.

"True," she said. Then, more quietly, she added, "I really do miss your Johnny Depp posters."

We both started giggling. "I miss them, too," I said.

AT BREAKFAST THE NEXT DAY, the four of us decided we'd go first to the police station to report the incident, and then we would take that visit to the Icelandic Horses that Beattie had promised me. She'd made it out like the trip was just for me, but I knew she was really excited to see the animals, too. After all, she was far more the horsewoman than I was. She'd even been taking riding lessons at one of the horse farms outside of Charlottesville, and while I knew nothing about horses, it seemed to me like she was getting pretty good.

The police officer on duty was respectful as we all gave our statements, and she promised she'd look into Ms. Weber and her employer. She also said she'd alert the other officers to the situation so that they could keep an eye on the situation while we were in the city. Given that we didn't know who Ms. Weber was, really, and had no information about where she was staying, we couldn't expect much more, not based on the feeling Beattie had gotten that she was in physical danger. But I did appreciate the officer taking the situation seriously.

Somehow, the fact that we had all been willing to give statements seemed to lift Beattie's spirits a bit. Maybe she felt more affirmed in her reaction, or maybe it was that she felt like the police were looking out for us. Whatever made her feel better, I was all for it.

One of Beattie's pet peeves as a seasoned world traveler was the way Americans dominated almost every situation we were in. She talked about the two Texans who had shouted to one another through the arches at Stonehenge one trip and the Oregonian who had insisted that the chef remake his noodles in Bangkok because the waiter couldn't assure him they were entirely vegan. So when she let out a loud "Yeehaw!" as we approached the pick-up location for the horse tour, I was surprised but also delighted. She was definitely in a good mood, and fortunately, the young man who was our driver appreciated her cowgirl enthusiasm and returned her call with a "Howdy!" of his own.

I, for my part, wanted to shrink into my peacoat and disappear, but Adaire and Aaran joined in with enthusiastic whoops all the rest of the way to where we saw long stables and short, stocky horses. Finally, I let out a little holler of my own. This was going to be fun.

And it was a blast. We got a short riding lesson that taught us the key phrases in Icelandic to bring the horses into each of their five gaits. I pretty much stuck with the slow stuff, but Beattie immediately took to the commands and set her horse racing after the guide as soon as we moved into the lava fields. Adaire and Aaran showed their own bursts of speed, but I was quite content to enjoy the natural beauty, chat with my adorable horse named Nico, and keep my balance.

Two Dutchmen were also on our tour, and they regaled us with their travel tales, all of which involved horses of some sort. They had decided they were going to ride horses in as many nations as possible. "Maybe you'll get a documentary like Ewan McGregor did with his motorcycle," Adaire joked.

"I feel certain that it helps to have been a co-star with both Nicole Kidman and Darth Vader if one wants to secure such an opportunity," one of the men said, and I didn't disagree.

The whole day was a blast, and when, after almost three hours of riding, we made it back to the stables, I was exhausted but in the best way. . . and I loved Nico. If I hadn't thought

Butterball would be jealous and that our host might frown on it, I would have probably offered to buy him. Instead, I contented myself with the fact that a young girl of about ten came out to take him from me and lead him to his stall after our ride. I couldn't take a horse from his girl, after all.

Both Adaire and I fell asleep, our heads propped together, on the ride back into the city center, so when we woke up at our drop-off location, I felt a bit disoriented. That feeling increased when I stepped out of the Land Rover and caught sight of a short, dark-haired woman looking at me from a nearby doorway. It was Erika Weber.

She stalked toward us as soon as the Land Rover pulled away, but I was able to alert Beattie in time for her to turn toward the woman. Our new Dutch friends also turned toward her after I shouted her name, so when the woman arrived, all six of us were facing her, and I was piping mad. I'd be damned if I'd let this woman ruin another stupendous day.

"You need to leave," I said and almost stomped my foot, like Nico, to emphasize my point.

"This is a public place," she said, gesturing around the small city square where we stood. "I have every right to be here as much as you do."

She sounded like Verruca Salt in *Willy Wonka and The Chocolate Factory*, and I hoped she'd fall down a garbage shaft. But instead, she just stood there and looked at me.

"We must talk about the book," she said.

"I told you that we are not discussing anything." I stood up straighter as I watched our Dutch friends circle behind Ms. Weber, effectively boxing her in. If she wasn't going to move along, then we were going to have this conversation on our terms, their action seemed to say. "You threatened Beattie, and we have reported your actions to the police."

She tsked and shook her head. "Such things are not necessary. Nor are they effective." She held out a business card. "I will meet you here at 6 p.m. Bring the book." As she turned to go, one of the men, whose name I remembered now as Hans, stepped right in front of her, and she slammed into his broad chest. "Excuse me," she said.

He quickly stepped away, a look of surprise on his face. Then Ms. Weber walked off as if she had just been out for a stroll in the city.

Hans looked at us. "She had a knife," he said, "against my stomach."

It looked like Beattie hadn't been wrong at all. "Going back to the police," she said, and we all marched after her.

Hans gave his statement to the same officer we'd seen earlier in the day, and this time, she looked even more concerned and promised she'd keep all of us informed about the investigation. As we stood to leave, she said, "I did begin this morning, but Ms. Weber is a very hard woman to find." She looked at me closely. "If you see her again, don't wait to come in."

I nodded as a promise to her and myself. I wasn't going to let this bully get away with her tactics. No way.

HANS AND HIS FRIEND, who in my head I kept calling Franz in a way I knew was juvenile but couldn't help, said goodbye outside the station, and we were back to our foursome, our starving foursome, it seemed. Horseback riding made a person hungry.

Tonight, though, I wasn't in the mood for fancy, so I suggested we find a pizza place. Fortunately, Aaran had already scoped one out, so we walked the few blocks to the restaurant and enjoyed the glow of the brick pizza ovens as we strategized.

"So the police can't find this woman," Adaire said, "but she seemingly has no problem finding us. I don't like it."

As the waiter set four very dark beers in front of us, Beattie said, "I don't like it either. I feel like we're being followed." She looked around the room.

A shiver ran down my spine. "She's definitely keeping an eye on us somehow." I suddenly looked at my bag. "Do you think she placed a tracking device on one of us?"

Beattie rolled her eyes, and Adaire grinned before growing serious. "I doubt it," he said, "but you never know, I guess."

I had really been joking, but his response made me nervous again, nervous enough to actually check my bag this time. The only thing in there was the fake dictionary with the book and my wallet, and when I ran my fingers along the seams, I didn't feel anything.

Beattie, despite her reaction a moment ago, emptied the contents of her purse on the table. Since we'd left BB in the very excited care of our host for the day, she was traveling even lighter than I was, with only her wallet and a tube of lipstick on hand. A quick search of possible hiding places in her bag turned up nothing as well.

When we looked at our dates with expectation in our eyes, they both turned out their pockets and showed us there was nothing suspicious. Short of disassembling our shoes, it looked like we had examined all the possible sources for a hidden device. Somehow, I didn't feel much better.

Unfortunately, my knowledge of surveillance was entirely derived from TV and movies, so I began imagining someone was listening with a parabolic microphone or had put out a code to alert them if Beattie's credit card was used. Within a few seconds, my brain was spiraling through a million options for how Weber had come to know where we'd be this afternoon.

When the pizza arrived, all rich with cheese, honey, basil, and chilis, I was brought back to reality. Tomato sauce and bread never failed to pull me back to earth, and it didn't fail now, thank goodness. I picked up a slice of the hand-tossed pizza and took a bite. The combination of the sweetness of the honey and the bite of the peppers was divine, and I completely believe it sparked my revelation. "What if she's just asking our host where we are?"

Beattie stopped with a slice halfway to her mouth and looked at me. "Could it be that easy?"

"I expect our host has more propriety than that," Adaire said. "Doesn't she?"

I shrugged. "Maybe she thinks that woman is a friend of ours." I finished my first slice and reached for another. "We'll just have to ask."

A truffle, potato, and ricotta pizza and two beers apiece later, we wandered back to our guesthouse to find our host, Elena, watching BB run in a makeshift play area she'd fashioned from cardboard boxes held to the ground with her furniture. He was in hamster heaven, it seemed, because every time he ran over to Elena, she gave him a peanut. I sighed. As if he weren't spoiled before.

To my surprise, Aaran folded his large frame into a seated position inside the play space and began to coax BB over. The tiny rodent sniffed his large hand and then ran right up his sleeve and took a seat on his neck, just below his long, black hair. At that point, he curled up and went to sleep just like he'd been invited into a four-star hotel after a long day of travel.

Aaran smiled and settled himself carefully against the cardboard that was propped against a wingback chair and closed his eyes in an act that appeared to be one of hamster-human solidarity. The rest of us went a little goo-goo-eyed, and I thought Beattie might ask the man to marry her right there.

Instead, we all headed into the small kitchen, where Elena made us decaf coffee and asked us about our day with the horses. We chatted a bit, and then I decided to broach our most pressing subject. "Elena, has anyone been asking about us? Maybe wondering where we're spending out time?"

Elena sat up very straight. "If they had been, I wouldn't have told them anything," she said with firmness. "The privacy of my guests is very important."

Adaire had been right. "Thank you. I only asked because someone has been following us and showed up at the end of our horse-riding tour, and we aren't sure how she found us." I sighed, disappointed that my brilliant idea hadn't panned out.

But then Elena's hand flew to her mouth. "Oh no, I have made a mistake." Tears pooled in her eyes. "Erika is not your friend?"

I tilted my head and looked at the woman. "Erika? Erika Weber?"

"Yes, she's staying in my third room. I thought you were all traveling together." She looked up at the ceiling and shook her head. "But you aren't, are you? I'm so stupid."

Beattie put her hand on the woman's arm. "You are not stupid, but why would you think we were all together?"

"Because when she arrived yesterday, she said you were, that she had come a bit later because of work but that you were meeting your friends. She knew all of your names," Elena's eyes were wide. "How would she know your names if she isn't your friend?"

I didn't point out that there were lots of ways to discover people's names because the woman was distraught and had no reason at all to disbelieve someone who knew the names of her guests. "It's okay. No harm done. But you said she's staying here. Why haven't we seen her?" I said as much to my friends as to our host.

"You haven't?" Elena said. "That is odd." She looked out the kitchen door to the dining room. "She hasn't been at breakfast when you are."

I shook my head.

"She has been keeping strange hours," Elena said with a furrow in her brow like she was trying to think through the comings and goings of her guests for the past few days. "Out very early and back very late. Still, it is not a big house." She waved an arm around the small house.

Beattie smiled. "It's a lovely house, but if you would, please don't talk about us with her again, would you?"

I was glad Beattie decided not to tell her that Weber had been threatening us. I didn't want to alarm our host or cause her to feel even more guilty than she already did.

"Absolutely not," Elena said. "Thank you for asking and for being so kind about my indiscretion." She smiled at each of us.

"Actually," Beattie continued, "please don't mention that you know about her, um, fabrication. It would be best if you just played along like you didn't know."

Elena studied Beattie for a minute and then gave a single nod. "Okay, Ms. Andrews, I will keep what you have said to myself." She stood. "Now, I have a favor of my own to ask. Can I keep BB again tomorrow? We have had such fun."

The four of us walked into the living room and found Aaran curled up on the floor with BB now tucked into his forearm.

"Of course," I said, "but you may have to wrestle him away from Aaran."

"That won't be necessary," Aaran said with his eyes still closed. "This little guy is cute, but he just ate the cuff off my sleeve." He slowly moved one arm out to reveal a frayed edge on the left arm of his shirt. "Must have been needing fiber," Aaran mumbled.

AFTER I SCOOPED Butterball off Aaran's arm, thereby saving his other shirt sleeve from trimming, Adaire and I made our way upstairs. I had briefly thought of suggesting we swap roommates, but I wasn't sure I was ready for that yet. And I definitely needed to talk about the idea with Beattie before I sprung it on her. So rather than inviting Adaire in, I led him to a small settee by the window that looked out over the end of the hall.

BB had stayed asleep when I'd set him in his bag, and now I put him down on the small side table near the sofa. He didn't even stir, and I wasn't sure if I was glad for the lack of distractions or wishing I had one.

I looked over at Adaire, and he took my hand. "Poe, it's been a long day. We have a lot to discuss about"—he looked down at our joined hands—"well, this. But there is time. I plan on sticking around if that's okay with you."

"More than okay," I said, "but yes, I need to be deliberate and thoughtful. And this mess with Weber has got me all discombobulated."

"Excellent word," he said as he leaned over and kissed me gently. "One of my favorites," he whispered as he pulled away.

"The word or . . ." I didn't finish.

"Or," he said as he helped me to my feet. "Until tomorrow." He kissed my cheek and then handed me BB. "I think it best, for the sake of all our shirts, if this guy sleeps in his cage tonight."

"Agreed," I said. "After all those peanuts, he might be in need of a lot more fiber. Newspaper is a better option for that sustenance."

Adaire smiled, and I waved as I closed the door with my foot and then did that thing that women do in movies and slid down to the floor with the door at my back.

Beattie came in soon after, and while I was a bit swoony, she looked thoroughly gobsmacked, and her lips were swollen. And our two ways of doing relationships seemed spot on—Beattie was going all in and a little wild, while I was subdued and probably too much in my head. But both of us were happy, and I loved that.

4

The following morning, the four of us sat down to breakfast on high alert. Beattie and I had both checked our door locks twice after going to bed, fairly certain that Weber was going to try to break in. And when I asked, Aaran said he had moved his bed against the door for the same reason. "I wanted her to try just a wee bit," he said.

I didn't disagree. I would have liked to have seen that.

"She never came in last night," Elena said as she set the most amazing omelet full of tomatoes and cheese in front of me. "I went to check on her this morning since I didn't see her, and she didn't ring if she came in after I locked up, but her room is empty."

"Like she took all her things?" I asked.

"Yes, Everything of hers is gone." Elena shook her head. "She must have left while I was at the store yesterday afternoon." She sighed and then smiled when she saw BB in his bag next to Beattie's tray. "If it's okay with you, I'd like to take Butterball to meet the children at the grade school around the corner. My friend is a teacher."

I looked at Beattie, and she nodded. "But it's probably best not to let the children hold him. He can be quite the escape artist."

"Oh, I would never. They have a cage for when the children bring in pets. My friend cleaned it today just in case we got your permission." Elena beamed and said, "May I?" as she reached for her furry friend.

"Of course," I said. "BB will love the outing, especially if it involves peanuts."

"I already promised that the children could give him treats." She blushed. "I hope I'm not doing more than I should."

"Trust us when we say you could not spoil that hamster more than we do," Beattie said.

At that moment, my phone rang, and I stepped into the living room to answer it.

"This is Inga. Are you available this morning?" the voice on the other end of the line said.

"Hi, Inga. Good morning," I said, trying to force a bit of casualness and manners into the call. "Yes, we are available to meet. What time?"

"Be ready in fifteen minutes. We are sending a car." She hung up.

I looked down at the phone in my hand. So much for the way that BB had broken the ice with her. Back to business, I supposed.

I went back into the room and told my friends that we had to eat quickly. Fortunately, we all managed to scarf down our meals before we heard the tinny beep of the horn outside. I ran upstairs, grabbed my bag, and retrieved the dictionary from where I'd tucked it under the far side of my mattress for the night. Not the most ingenious hiding place, but better than nothing, I had figured.

When I jogged back down the stairs, Adaire whisked me through the door and threw his jacket over my shoulders in the same motion. For just a second, I felt like a movie star, and

I let myself get carried away as he opened my door and then slid in next to me. I waved to the people we passed on the street from behind the sunglasses I had spontaneously grabbed, and when Beattie, yet again, rolled her eyes at me, I turned my wave into one the queen would envy and spent the rest of the time fawning over "my fans" on the streets of Reykjavik. I'm sure the driver thought I was just another wild American, and he wasn't wrong . . . at least not at that moment.

A few minutes later, we pulled up in front of a nondescript house on a residential street. The home was made of white plaster and stood two stories tall. Window boxes with what looked like tiny fir trees adorned each window, but beyond that, I couldn't see anything spectacular about this particular house.

The driver told Aaran he had been paid, so we stepped onto the street and turned toward the house he'd noted. As soon as we reached the short rise of steps, the door opened, and a man in a suit waited for us to approach. "Welcome, Ms. Baxter, Ms. Andrews, Mr. Anderson, and Mr. Anderson," he said as we walked past him. "May I take your coats?"

I slipped Adaire's jacket from my shoulders and handed it to the man, wondering if I was meeting my first real-life butler. When he had left the room, I looked at Beattie.

"Jeeves?" she said in a terrible English accent, and this time, Aaran rolled his eyes.

A moment later, Inga stepped out from a doorway to the right of the front door and said, "Please join us in the library." She was stern, but I couldn't tell if she was *more* stern or if somber was just her natural way.

We followed her through the beautiful wooden door, and when we stepped inside, I gasped. The walls were covered from floor to ceiling with books set in fine wooden shelving that looked, I thought, to be made of mahogany. High-backed chairs sat near the furthest wall of shelves, and just in front of us, a beautiful wood table was surrounded by seven simple chairs that, somehow, conveyed luxury even through their clean lines.

I sat down in the chair Gunnar pointed to after he shook my hand, and while everyone settled in, I let myself marvel at the stunning chandelier, mullioned windows, and lush Oriental rug under my feet. The books on the shelves closest to us looked to be from a variety of time periods and covered a gamut of genres. I saw a James Michener mass-market paperback on one shelf and a full set of Thomas Carlyle's works in what looked to be original leather bindings just beside it. This was, I could tell, a book lover's library—the space created by someone who loved books both as stories and as artifacts. It was my idea of paradise.

"Thank you for coming," Gunnar said.

I pried my eyes from the room and said, "Thank you for having us. And thank you for your help the other night."

He smiled, but the expression didn't reach his eyes. Quietly, he said, "Yes, that was most unfortunate. I take it you've had no further trouble."

The four of us exchanged a glance, and Beattie finally said, "Well, actually, Erika Weber appears to be stalking us." She explained about Weber's appearance at the horseback tour drop-off and about how we found out she had been staying in the same place we were. "She seems to have cleared out now," Beattie finished, "but I don't expect we've seen the last of her."

Inga and Gunnar exchanged another glance, and this time, I wasn't willing to ignore it. "Do you know something about her?" I asked. "Have you had dealings with her before?"

After receiving a small nod from Inga, Gunnar sighed and said, "We have, unfortunately. Her employer is a man 'with connections,' as I think you might say in America."

"He's a mobster?" I almost shouted. "Like Al Capone?"

"I do not know who Al Capone is, but yes, a sort of organized crime lord. His name is Finneas Swagley, and from time to time, his path and ours cross." Gunnar looked at Inga again. "The president has worked with law enforcement time and again to try to apprehend him, but to no avail."

I could feel it coming, the weight of the impending request already making the air heavier and denser, and to my surprise, I wasn't scared. In fact, I felt a little exhilarated. "How can we help?"

Inga smiled, and once again, I found I really liked this woman despite her sometimes-grumpy demeanor. "I felt confident you would be willing if we asked, and here, we didn't even have to ask."

Adaire put a hand on my arm. "Poe, really, this could be dangerous."

"It could be, but then it seems like we're already in danger. And we don't know exactly what we're being asked to do." I put my hand over his. "Let's hear them out before we decide."

Beattie nodded, and while her face appeared serious, I could see a hint of a smile at one corner of her mouth. She was as excited as I was.

"Before we suggest our plan, might we do a bit of business first? I think it would make us all feel better to have the book securely held in our vault as we play a bit of cat and mouse," Gunnar said with a small smile of his own.

"Absolutely," I said as I took the fake dictionary from my bag and opened it. "I presume this means you have confirmed the book's authenticity?"

"Beyond any shadow of a doubt," Inga said. "It is just as you described it, and you can be assured you made a wise purchase."

I hadn't realized how much anxiety I was carrying about the possibility that I had been duped until she alleviated the concern. My shoulders dropped two inches. "Excellent," I said.

When we concluded business, Inga stepped into the

hallway to ask the butler to bring in coffee and pastries for us. "A small celebration," Inga said.

I was thrilled to have more coffee, and I was never one to turn down a pastry. But I was also very eager to hear about what I was already calling our "sting operation" in my mind. I had visions of stakeouts with bad convenience store coffee and dead drops on benches in parks. I thought we might have to wear wires or set up clandestine meets in old warehouses. Never mind that I hadn't seen a single convenience store in Reykjavik, nor an old warehouse. This was how these things worked; I knew it.

It seemed this was not, however, how things worked when the president of a nation was involved. Rather, we were going to simply omit some information from our story and see what Erika Weber did next. Inga put it this way. "We'd like you to simply act like we were not able to come to a deal and let her approach you again."

"Okay, I can lie," I said with perhaps too much enthusiasm. "Then what?"

"Then you ask for her plans for the book. See you if you can find out what her employer's intentions are," Gunnar said.

"All right," I said, "And if he simply wants the book for his collection?" I was having trouble figuring out exactly what they hoped to gain from what would be a completely legal transaction if we hadn't just made the sale.

"That's fine," Inga said. "It's a look into his operation that we are seeking. Here's where it gets tricky." She held my gaze. "You must ask to be paid in cash."

I stared at her for a moment and then shook my head. "Why would I do that? It wouldn't be safe to travel with that kind of money on hand."

"You're right," Gunnar continued as he leaned forward. "But if you were planning on skimming some from the top before you paid your employer . . ." He didn't finish his statement.

"I'd need cash so that I could hide the total sale price," I said as understanding dawned. "You want me to see if they'll recruit me?" My emotion was quickly turning from excitement to fear.

Inga nodded. "Yes. If you have a few days more to spend in Iceland, we'd like to see if you can get yourself into Swagley's operation as an expert."

I looked at Beattie, whose eyes were wide, and I made sure not to meet Adaire's eyes, although I could see him shaking his head out of my peripheral vision.

"So I'd be a book-buying double agent?" I asked. "Could my code name be Double-o-Book?"

Beattie's face broke into a smile. She loved James Bond, and I knew the idea of being a spy would appeal to her.

"Sure," Inga said with a roll of her eyes. "Does that mean you'll do it?"

Now, I finally looked at Adaire, who seemed entirely displeased. "It might be a good part of my cover if you really hate this idea. Keep you free and clear and add a little nuance to the story."

He groaned. "At least I won't have to lie," he said.

"We're in," I said at that. "What do we do first?"

THE PLAN TURNED out to be fairly simple. We were just supposed to act dejected when we left, talk loudly about needing to find a new buyer, have Adaire put out the word about the book through his channels just to add authenticity, and then sit back and wait.

Adaire was assured that his supervisors would be informed, by the president himself, about the operation so that he wouldn't be suspected of anything untoward, and that seemed to appease some of his nerves.

It was only after the plan was all set that I realized Aaran hadn't said a word during the whole meeting. "You okay with all this?" I asked him as I glanced at Beattie.

She turned to him also, saying, "Yeah, you okay?" She leaned over and looked him in the eye to be sure.

He nodded and then looked over at me. "Poe, this could be dangerous. You know that, right?" When his gaze shifted to Beattie, his eyes softened. "For you, too, beautiful."

I saw Beattie swallow, but she held his eyes and said, "I know. But we can handle ourselves, and with two dashing men as backup, what could go wrong?"

Everyone smiled then except Aaran, whose face grew even more somber. But he didn't say anything further, and I got the impression he wouldn't. So we made our plan about how to be in contact: a message left with the barista at the coffee shop up the street from our guesthouse, as close to a dead drop as I was going to get. Then we were on our way.

Our performance began as soon as we stepped outside. I hung my head and tucked the dictionary up under my chin. Beattie muttered to herself about promises and disappointments. For his part, Adaire hurried ahead with his phone to his ear and called his boss to ask her to help us locate a new buyer and to see if the Library of Scotland might be interested in the volume.

Aaran was even more quiet than usual, though, and once I'd made what I felt was enough of a show, I sidled back next to him to ask if he was okay. He shook his head once, "Not here," he murmured.

I looked at him sharply, but I didn't press further. He'd tell us what was going on with him when he was ready, I figured, and for now, we had the part of excited tourists to play.

After I made a phone call to Uncle Fitz to tell him the deal had fallen through, a ruse he had already been made aware of by Inga and Gunnar's people, we decided, very loudly, that we had done all we could do for the moment and were going to make the best of the situation and do some sightseeing.

I had been dying to see some turf houses, so we made a plan to go out to the Arbaer Museum to get a glimpse. Fortunately, it was easy enough to get to by bus, our trusty smartphones said, so we made our way to the appropriate stop and climbed aboard.

Unlike the thatched roof cottages of southwest England, which were the closest things I'd seen to turf houses before—and they weren't very similar at all to the thatched houses, in fact—almost no Icelanders lived in turf houses anymore. The earthen-roofed buildings were still preserved at Arbaer, though, and I loved our time wandering among the buildings.

Fortunately for us, it wasn't just turf houses at the museum but houses from various periods. Knowing I was going to be interested in reading every word about every building, I wandered off on my own and took photos, sending a few via email to Paisley Sutton, an architectural salvage expert back home, because I knew she'd love them. The number of exclamation points in her response told me I was right.

I was just taking a rest with my back against a turf-covered sheep's house when someone sat down next to me. Expecting to see Beattie or Adaire, I opened my mouth to rave about the museum and then felt it fall further open when I saw Erika Weber, in jeans and a cable-knit sweater, sitting next to me.

"I hear you've had a disappointing day, Ms. Baxter," she said as she tapped the book in my bag that was now between us.

Instinctively, I pulled the bag free and moved it to my other side. "I don't know what you mean," I said, deciding on the spur of the moment to play up my desire to avoid working with her. That seemed plausible since surely Gunnar and Inga would have warned me away from her.

"Now, now," she said with a purr that reminded me of the cats from 1,001 Dalmatians, "let's be honest from here on, shall we? You know I have been following you, and I know that the president did not, after all, decide to purchase the book."

I wasn't surprised that she knew this information, but I was a bit put off by the speed at which she had taken action. Her boss might really want this book, which might just play to my benefit.

I decided to keep playing it cool and just stared off across the field before me.

"We are prepared to pay you double what you paid for the book," Weber said after a few moments of silence. "I think you'll agree that is more than fair."

I took a deep breath and looked down at my bag, hoping I wasn't overacting. "I need to see what other buyers express interest," I said.

"Oh, I can assure you. I will be your only offer in Iceland." Her voice was cold and tight. "And we know your uncle prefers that the book stays here." She patted my arm. "You can make us and your uncle happy quite easily."

I finally allowed myself to look at her, and her casual grin made goosebumps rise on my skin. "I'll need to talk about it with my partner."

Erika stood up and offered me a hand to follow. "Please do, but know we won't wait long."

"What does that mean exactly?" I asked.

"Take our offer. Or don't. By tomorrow," she said and made her way across the field toward, well, nothing. I had to admit that was really spooky, and for a minute, I wondered if she was going to be scooped up by an alien spaceship. Then I saw a sleek black car pull out from behind a rise and drive toward her. I wasn't sure that was less creepy than a UFO.

I hurried back to the middle of the museum space and looked around for my friends. Beattie saw me from where she was sitting and making a video on her phone. She had built up quite an Instagram following, and while I didn't understand the medium, I loved that she was enjoying herself.

When she stopped filming, she made her way over to me. "This place is amazing! So full of stories and history," she said.

I nodded, but I couldn't bring myself to talk casually about history after the encounter I'd just had.

"What's wrong?" Beattie said as she took in my silence. "You okay?"

I shook my head. "Erika Weber just offered me a deal."

Beattie spun around three times, looking for Weber.

"She's gone," I said and pointed in the direction the car had driven across the field. "I have to give her a decision by tomorrow."

"Or what?" Beattie asked.

"I asked the same thing," I said. "She didn't answer."

ONCE WE LOCATED Aaran and Adaire, who had been exploring the sweet shop at the museum, I explained what had happened and the timeline for our response. I didn't say anything more in case someone was listening, which seemed, at this point, very likely.

Aaran listened and then said, "You should sell."

I studied his face for a moment, waiting for a wink or nod to tell me he was playing into our performance. But his face stayed like stone, and I felt my skin prickle again. He definitely knew more than he was sharing.

"Do you have any other leads?" I asked as I turned to Adaire.

He shook his head. "The library isn't interested, and my boss couldn't recommend anyone who didn't have ties to the Icelandic government." He sighed. "I'm afraid to say this may be your only option for recouping your uncle's investment."

I nodded as if I was thinking it over. "I don't like her, and she's totally creepy. But her offer is a good one." I lowered my voice for effect. "And maybe we could make a little something off the deal."

Beattie frowned at me but then nodded. Adaire shook his head. "Leave me out of any of that," he said. "I'm not interested."

"Fair enough," I said. "I'll let her know."

"I'll pass along the word," said a tall, thin man in a rain slicker and khakis from the next table over as he stood and walked out the door.

I stared at my friends and shivered. "That was downright scary."

Aaran said quietly. "It's only going to get worse."

"Well, that's not foreboding at all," Beattie said with a nervous chuckle. "You all ready? I could use a relaxing dinner by the fire."

We all agreed and decided to splurge on a cab back to our rooms. When we arrived, the golden lights in the windows let something release inside me. It wasn't home, but it was homey, and I'd take homey.

That warm feeling subsided as soon as I stepped in the door, however, because there, in the hallway, was Elena, and she was very, very dead.

5

I know I didn't imagine the look of frustration on the police officer's face when she arrived and saw the four of us for the third time. "Hello," she said and walked past where we stood in the front garden, as we'd been directed by the first officers on the scene.

There hadn't been any need to check Elena's vitals since we could see the knife in her chest and the blood from the wound, so we hadn't even gone fully into the house. Instead, Adaire had called the police from his phone, and we had stood shivering in the yard waiting for, thankfully, just a few moments.

I told the first officer and three officers after that, including our "friend"—whose name I finally learned was Officer Jonsdottir—that we had come back after a day out and found her like this when we returned. The door had been unlocked as usual, and neither my friends nor I had noticed anything unusual.

After Elena's body was cleared from the room, Officer Jonsdottir told us we'd have to find a new place to stay since this was now a crime scene. She recommended another home a few blocks away and sent an officer up with us so we could collect our things.

"I'll be in touch if we find anything out," she said as she walked with us to the street. "Normally, I would think this was a robbery, but given what has been happening with you, I fear foul play."

I nodded because, well, I couldn't disagree.

"Have you had any further contact with Ms. Weber?" she asked me.

I almost told her the whole situation, but Aaran stepped up and said, "No, nothing since we told you about our encounter yesterday. Right, Poe?"

Officer Jonsdottir looked from him to me, and I could tell she sensed something was off. But I went along with Aaran. "Not a word. Hopefully, she's cleared out." I looked back at the house. "This does seem too odd to be a coincidence, though."

The officer nodded. "I have your numbers and will be in touch," she said as she turned back to the house.

"Oh, wait," Beattie shouted as she turned back. "Our hamster."

"Excuse me?" Officer Jonsdottir said. "Did you say hamster? As in the rodent?"

"Yes," Beattie said as she tried to get around the officer into the house. "Elena was pet-sitting him while we were out. He must still be inside."

"Please wait here," Officer Jonsdottir said as she signaled for two other officers to join her.

A few moments later, they returned without BB. "I'm sorry. There is no hamster anywhere that we can see."

"Oh no! He must have escaped from his bag. Did you see a thick plastic bag about this big?" She held her hands out to mimic the size of a small purse.

"No, nothing like that either," one of the men who had searched said.

I could see Beattie's breaths coming faster, and a look of panic was forming in her eyes. I was worried, too, but I didn't have nearly as much of my heart tucked into that tiny hamster body as my best friend did. "Beattie, we'll find him." I turned to the officers. "Do you mind if we take a quick look?"

Officer Jonsdottir nodded. "I'll go with you."

The three of us scoured high and low, but there was no sign of BB or his bag. I didn't want to think it, but I knew it was true. "The murderer took our hamster," I said in a whisper.

Beattie started to hyperventilate, and Officer Jonsdottir helped her outside onto the stoop, where Beattie put her head between her knees and took deep breaths.

"Please put that in your report," I said. "He's very special to us, and we want him found. I'll even offer a reward." I didn't really have substantial cash for such a reward, but given the scheme we'd launched with Inga and Gunnar, I might be able to get some help there. "Okay?"

Officer Jonsdottir nodded. "Of course." She sat down beside Beattie. "I have a cat. Her name is Astrid, and I love her like my child. We will find Butterball." She rubbed small circles on Beattie's back, and I saw my friend begin to breathe more easily.

The two women stood a few moments later, and then Adaire and Aaran took our bags and loaded them into the cab going to our new guesthouse. On the way there, Aaran instructed the driver to take a route that wound through Reykjavik by saying we just wanted to relax and see the city a bit. It was a nice cover, and it was relaxing. It was also hopefully enough to shake any tails we had so that we could feel confident in our new lodgings.

When we finally arrived, the new place was nice but truly not as lovely as Elena's place had been. Of course, nowhere would have been, not after our host had been murdered . . . apparently because of us.

Aaran checked us in under the fake names we'd quietly selected on the drive—Patricia Bannister, Beatrice Hampshire, and Alan and Amos Alexandran. Then he inquired about other guests, saying that I had a bit of a social phobia and needed to prepare to meet new people. I sat with my face turned in a chair away from the desk, trying to act far shyer and much more nervous than I naturally was.

The gentlemen who owned the cottage assured us we were the only guests. "And we only have two rooms, so no one else will be coming during your stay," he added.

I let out a long sigh of relief, if not for the reason our host expected, and followed at the end of our little train of people to our rooms on the second floor. They were quaint and well-kept, with reading chairs and lots of light, and while I missed the bookish snugness of Elena's space, I was glad we had a new place to stay that was personal and calming.

Much to my delight, which I kept tamped down, the host said he and his husband would be delighted if we brought dinner in to eat in their sitting room by the fire, so Aaran, in a knit cap and high-collared jacket to help him look a bit less noticeable, ducked out to a local place and got us burgers—lamb burgers in fact—and French fries that were fried dark and crispy, just like I loved them.

While we ate, our hosts stepped out for the evening to see a string ensemble play, they said, so we had the house to ourselves. Still, we were all nervous at being overhead, so I put my phone onto some Guns N' Roses, turned it up, and then set it near us to hopefully drown out our voices if someone was listening in.

We had a lot to discuss, but my most pressing question was for Aaran. "Okay, what do you know?" I asked after I had devoured half of the most amazing burger I'd ever eaten, even though it was lamb.

Aaran looked at me and sighed. "I've had run-ins with

Swagley's people before . . . in my work." He shrugged as he looked over at his brother. "The world of fishermen is pretty small."

Adaire nodded. "So what happened?"

"I always steered clear, but a couple of guys I've worked with have violated catch limits and such so that they could sell to Swagley. Black market catches mostly. Totally shady." Aaran took another bite of his burger. "The guy is just really bad news. One of those men I was talking about . . . he disappeared."

The bite of French fry that I was chewing stuck in my throat. "You mean Swagley had him killed?"

Aaran shrugged again. "I can't say for sure, but yeah, I think so." He wasn't exactly nonchalant about this whole story, but given the rate at which he was eating his food, I could tell he wasn't exactly torn up about it either.

"Why didn't you say something?" Beattie said.

"I wasn't sure how. You two seemed so excited about the prospect of playing spy, and to be honest, I thought the Icelandic government would offer some protection or something. But now Poe's being targeted when she's alone, and they've kidnapped your hamster." His voice got louder as he spoke.

Beattie waved her hand to suggest he lower his voice. "Now that you say that, maybe we should ask Gunnar and Inga for some protection from the government."

Aaran shook his head. "Do that, and you'll be in more danger. It's best to carry on with the plan and see if Poe can make her way in."

"Are you sure?" Adaire said. "This is sounding quite dangerous."

I looked over at Adaire, realizing I'd begun thinking of him as my boyfriend, and found it awfully cute that he was being so chivalric in his nerdy feminist way. "I'm okay with going forward. Aaran's right. I'm already in. Any change in tactic will put us all in more danger."

Beattie almost whispered. "And they have BB."

"And they have BB," I said as I leaned over and put my hand on her knee. "We'll get him back." I had no idea how we were going to do that. I wasn't even all that certain Weber and Swagley had our hamster. Kidnapping a hamster?

"The way you two fawn over that little guy," Aaran said, "it's no wonder they took him as collateral."

"The way *they* fawn over him?" Adaire said. "I seem to remember a certain fisherman napping with said hamster just yesterday."

Adaire said it as a joke, but the memory hit me hard as I thought about Elena and her warm living room. Thinking of that kind woman made me even more determined to follow through. If these people had killed her, I couldn't let them get away with it.

But that brought up a question, and I couldn't help but voice it. "Why would they kill Elena?"

Aaran shook his head. "Maybe she tried to protect BB."

Beattie gasped. "Oh, that precious woman. What a hero!"

I loved our hamster, but I wasn't sure saving him was worth risking your life. But then again, I wasn't sure the chance to kidnap him was worth killing for. I didn't say any of this, of course. If Beattie needed Elena to be our hamster's hero, so be it. I wasn't really willing to believe that, though.

"What's next then?" Adaire asked.

As if on cue, my phone rang. I answered after the first ring and heard Weber's voice on the other end of the line. "Tomorrow, meet us at 10 a.m." She named a location. "Your friends may come," she said.

I almost laughed at the opposite of the standard "come alone" requirement from other ransom situations. But I managed to hold the guffaw back behind a cough, then said, "Please be sure Butterball has plenty to eat."

"We've given him his own sofa. He's fine," she said and then hung up.

I stared at my phone for a moment, trying to figure out if the sofa comment had been serious or a sarcastic joke.

"Do they have him?" Beattie shouted.

I nodded. "He's fine, though." I hoped I was right. "They want to meet tomorrow." I relayed the rest of the demands. "I guess we know what's next now."

Aaran nodded. "We can go have breakfast at the coffee shop and leave word," he said. "Maybe they'll provide some protection, just for the meeting, without being obvious."

I sighed. "I hope so." A quick search told me that the location Weber had given me was in a small park just a few blocks away. "At least we're meeting in the open. They can have the police keep an eye on us."

"Speaking of which," Adaire said, "Do you think we should have told Officer Jonsdottir?"

Aaran shook his head. "We were definitely being watched, and my guess is she knows the situation. She seems to be quite the savvy lass."

I looked over at Beattie, but she wasn't taking any of this in. She looked exhausted—pale and drawn—and I decided to call it a night. "Gentlemen, I think we're going to bed. We can strategize further in the morning." I turned off the music on my phone, which had changed from GnR to The Commodores. "Beattie, you ready?"

Beattie nodded and then let Aaran kiss her cheek when they both stood up. He put his arm through hers and led her up the stairs. Adaire and I followed behind, our arms similarly interlocked. It was a quiet goodnight outside our rooms, and not just because someone might have been listening.

. . .

THE NEXT MORNING, the sun was bright and warm, and the soft yellow color of our room's walls made the whole space fairly glow. I woke before Beattie and slipped into the shower, hoping to let her sleep as long as she could. But when I came out, she was sitting up in bed with her clothes laid out beside her.

I took one look at her selection and smiled. "Feeling better?"

She scooped up the black leggings, hot pink sweater, and pink and green scarf. "Not really better, but determined." She winked at me and went into the bathroom.

When she came out, her hair was in a perfect twist, with the scarf tied jauntily around the front. She'd done her makeup style somewhere between a pin-up and a 1950s runway model, and as she sat on the bed to put on her knee-length stiletto boots, she smiled. "Let's go catch the bad guys."

"Okay, but first, I need you to do my hair and makeup. No way I'm showing up for this meeting looking all plain Jane," I said.

"You got it, sister," she said and proceeded to cream and lotion my hair until the curls were soft but solid. She did my makeup with waves of blue across my eyes over cat-eye liner, and I looked like I was one of *Charlie's Angels* but with hips, less finesse, and a whole lot more attitude. It was perfect.

When I walked outside, I decided that I could live in Iceland, mostly because the dry, cool air was perfect for my hair, but also, the people were nice, the food was good, and it never got very hot. I really hated the heat, and unfortunately, Charlottesville was a sweltering bowl of humidity and heat from May to September. Ugh. Icelandic weather and my Iceland-tempered hair suited me.

I tried to distract myself as we walked to the coffee shop to let our barista spy know about our meeting. Thoughts of how I might take Icelandic lessons and study Icelandic folklore at the university filled my mind, and I wondered if I might even begin to like fish if I lived here. That one was highly doubtful, but the disgust at the thought of me eating seafood was nicely distracting.

After I ordered our coffees and used our purposefully silly code phrase—"We have the package"—and passed the note with the meeting location and time to the server with my money, I made my way back to our table and waited. I thought I was just waiting for my coffee and some fruit pastry thing that made me feel like I was eating healthily when really the fruit was candied and not at all healthy.

But a few moments later, Officer Jonsdottir came in and headed right for us. I kind of wanted to scream and shoo her away, but I figured that would look even more suspicious than just sitting with the police officer who was handling the case of the woman who was murdered in our guesthouse.

Apparently, she felt the same way because when she sat down, she said, "We're talking about the investigation of your host's murder." The comment sounded forceful, as if she needed to command our attention to the matters at hand, but I knew she was just making sure we knew that she knew. A wave of relief passed over me.

"My usual," she said as the barista dropped off our coffees and pastries and a very large cup of coffee. "This is my usual spot."

I smiled and admired the way she closed her eyes to take her first sip. This woman appreciated coffee, and any coffee lover was a friend of mine.

"We haven't made any headway on BB's location, but we did receive this email this morning." She slid a single page across the table so that both Beattie and I could see it.

The hamster is safe and well-cared for. When we have what we want, we will return him unharmed.

Beneath the text was a photo of BB in front of a bowl of blueberries with today's paper beside him.

I laughed out loud. "This is proof of life," I said as I looked at Beattie.

She, however, was not laughing. "I hope they aren't feeding him too much fruit. It gives him stomach trouble."

I didn't dare point out to my distressed bestie that a little indigestion was the least of BB's worries, so I just patted her hands. "He looks good," I said.

She nodded half-heartedly before looking up at Office Jonsdottir. "What do they want?"

The officer shook her head and said, "We don't know." She sounded so sincere that I thought maybe she really didn't know. But then she said, "It's a familiar saga—kidnapping, ransom with unclear demands."

The word *saga* was a very particular word for this situation, and I got her meaning exactly. She knew precisely what was going on, and she wanted us to know she knew.

I couldn't get any words out, but fortunately, Aaran was quick to respond. "Really? A lot of people make ransom demands without naming their demands."

Officer Jonsdottir smiled. "You'd be surprised." She shook her head. "Once, a man demanded that he be given what, and I quote, 'I've been asking for from my father for years,' before he'd let his sister out of their family mansion north of the city."

"Did he make that demand of his father?" Adaire asked.

"No," the officer said with an even broader smile. "They asked it of their sister, who was seven at the time, the child of their father's second marriage. She had no idea what he wanted, but fortunately, she also thought her kidnapping was a big game and was none the wiser when we stormed in and 'saved' her. She was eating cake."

I laughed, and even Beattie cracked a smile. "Criminal mastermind, that guy," she said.

"Precisely," the police officer said before she grew more stern. "But unfortunately, in this situation, we have less to go on. Our IT department is looking into the source of the email, so that's a good lead."

"I suppose, though, that you don't have the resources of several massive government agencies at your disposal like on TV," I said, hoping to keep levity in the conversation but also ferret out a bit more info.

"Alas, no. It'll take us a couple of days at least, even with all the tremendous resources we have at our disposal." She looked down at the table. "But we are doing everything we can, and we will keep you closely updated."

I wasn't sure if that last sentence was code or a simple statement of fact, but I felt better just knowing she was here. "Thanks," I said. "I'm afraid we have to go. Got some appointments as tourists this morning."

She stood and picked up her gigantic paper coffee cup. "I'll be in touch," she said and headed out the door before us, another smart move on her part since now she wouldn't be thought to be lingering in order to follow us.

I downed my coffee and snagged a pastry before leading our party of four out the door. I felt like the drum major out in front of a band. I was tempted to try to do that thing the HBCU drum majors do where I high-stepped and spun around, but it would not have been pretty with my pastry. Not at all.

Instead, I just walked straight ahead and tried to look confident. I didn't feel confident, but sometimes, as they say, faking it is making it. The entire time I walked toward the park, I remembered my marching band instructor, Mr. Nail, and his instructions on how to heel-to-toe our feet so that our walk was smooth. It worked because when we turned into the park, I was much calmer and also very focused on how much the tendons in the top of my feet hurt, just like they did when I was in high school. Well, worse. Much worse, in fact.

When I saw Weber on a bench near the park entrance, I forgot all about my feet and clasped my bag to my chest for comfort. I hoped, after the fact, that the gesture looked protective, but given that I was protecting a stack of chopped-up newspaper hidden in the fake dictionary, I wasn't feeling very cautious about the material in the bag. Instead, I was just hoping it might stop a bullet if need be.

"I'm glad to see you, Ms. Baxter. And you, too, Ms. Andrews, Mr. Anderson, and Mr. Anderson. Thank you for coming." She gestured to the park bench beside her as if we were in a boardroom. It was weird.

Not knowing quite what else to do, I sat down, my bag still cradled against my chest. "I'm still not sure about this," I said. "But since you have BB . . ." I didn't know how to finish that sentence. I loved my pet, but I was having a hard time believing someone would actually think I'd go into business with an organized crime boss to save my hamster.

"We do, and he is fine." She looked up at Beattie. "I assure you. He is living quite the life in our care." She looked back at me. "Your friend is very distressed. So let us finish our business, and then we can have your beloved pet back to you in an hour."

It was then that I realized Weber's plan was more conniving than I thought. She wasn't banking on me making a deal to save BB. She was confident I'd make the deal to help Beattie, and she wasn't wrong. I'd do anything for my best friend, even put myself in grave danger, as I was about to do right now.

"I'm willing to sell, but I want to meet your boss, Mr. Swagley, I believe. I will only sell to him personally." My voice was trembling when I said it, but I knew it was what I needed to do. If I could get close to him, I might be able to help the president catch him. "And I need to be paid in cash."

Weber sat back and flicked her nails against each other. "Those are large demands, Ms. Baxter. May I ask your reasons?"

I was fortunate that Beattie and I had run through potential responses as she did my hair this morning because I didn't hesitate. "First, I want to meet your boss because I want to be sure he understands the value of what he is buying. I only sell, on principle, to people who understand the immense importance of books like these."

Weber nodded. "And the reason for cash?"

At this question, I looked down and tried to seem embarrassed. "I'm not getting paid very much, and we would like to enjoy our time abroad a bit more," I said with a quick glance at my friends. "Cash will allow me to make a small withdrawal before depositing the rest and transferring it to my uncle."

"So, in other words," Weber said, "you'd like us to pretend, for your sake, that we wanted to do the deal in cash, as a favor, so to speak."

"I hadn't thought of it that way, but yes, I suppose so." My hands were shaking as I spoke.

"Very well, I can arrange both of those things. Cash works better for us anyway, untraceable that way." She smiled and turned her body more fully in my direction. "May I please see the book?"

I hadn't anticipated this development and almost froze. Fortunately, Aaran was very quick on his feet and said, "You don't think we'd bring it with us in a public setting like this, do you?"

My eyes darted from him to Weber to see if she was frustrated, but she seemed, as always, completely calm. "Very well, but before you are allowed to see my employer, I will need to see the book. I can't give you access to him without the merchandise, you understand?"

I nodded quickly. I understood very well. We had to get the book back to make this work. "Absolutely. You'll be in touch, I assume," I said as I stood up.

"Of course. Look for my call in one hour." At that, she stood and walked away as if she were simply out strolling in the park for the day.

The four of us turned in the opposite direction and headed

toward a café nearby. I was fairly certain we were being followed, but I couldn't tell for sure. Still, we didn't take any chances and avoided all incriminating conversations while we ordered lunch. As soon as we had our food order placed, I excused myself to the bathroom and sent Inga a frantic text telling her we needed the book. She called me immediately.

"Can't give you the original, but we've created a very good copy. Where are you?"

I gave her the name of the café, and she moved her mouth away from the phone and spoke to someone I could vaguely hear in the background.

"There's a back door there. Ask your server for more napkins in ten minutes, and we'll take care of the rest." She hung up.

I stared at my phone a moment, then flushed and stepped back into the main part of the bathroom, where I found Beattie reapplying her lipstick.

"What?" she said. "We could very well have had someone listening to you, couldn't we? Besides, aren't women supposed to go to the bathroom together?" She rolled her eyes and dabbed her lips. "Ready?"

I nodded and followed her back to our table. For the next nine minutes, I forced myself to eat something that resembled a Reuben but wasn't quite that. The bread was amazing, and eventually, just to keep myself busy, I reverted to my childhood practice of taking something apart before eating it. Then I ate the bread.

Exactly ten minutes after Inga's instructions, I waved our waitress over and asked for more napkins. Since we had four perfectly good ones on the table, she gave me a bit of a weird look but came back a few minutes later with a huge stack of napkins that she handed directly to me with a sharp nod of her head. "As you requested," she said.

I dropped the stack into my lap and slid the fake book into

my bag while pretending to rummage for a pen. When I had indeed located the pen, I spread out the napkins and drew a mountain scene, again relying on the gifts of my younger days to occupy me. It was the best I could come up with as a reason for all the things that had just transpired.

My friends, bless their kind hearts, followed suit, and soon, we were all scribbling on napkins as we waited for Weber's call. I couldn't risk explaining the situation, but I appreciated that they all trusted me enough to just follow my lead.

Adaire drew a very respectable tiger head, and Aaran sketched some sort of seascape that felt perhaps just a wee bit too on-brand for him. Beattie, of course, had to outdo us all and created a completely symmetrical mandala pattern with various patterns and shading throughout the form. I wanted to frame her napkin art and hang it in my office at Uncle Fitz's shop.

But before I had a chance to compliment her, my phone rang. When I answered, Weber said, "Ten minutes, the café across the street."

I hung up and relayed the information to my friends, and we passed a silent look that said the equivalent of "so we are being watched." I could only hope that my sleight of hand was good enough when it came to getting the book into my bag.

6

This timeline gave us just enough time to speed-walk to our accommodation to keep up the ruse that the book wasn't on me. I ran up the stairs to our room, and just in case, I crouched down beside the bed, out of view of the window, and slipped the book into the dictionary safe before putting it back in my bag and standing up.

When I jogged back downstairs to meet my friends, I was sweaty and out of breath. Now, I just had to hope that our performance was believable enough . . . maybe the perspiration and panting would help sell it.

We hurried back to the café Weber had indicated, and as soon as we walked in, two men met us at the door and gestured toward the back of the restaurant. There, I saw a curtain hanging in one corner and thought immediately of Joel's club in the show *Marvelous Mrs. Maisel,* but I suspected these gangsters weren't Chinese. At least, I didn't imagine Swagley to be Chinese.

I expected to meet a German man, someone with an accent akin to Weber's, but instead, a thin, reedy guy who resembled Benedict Cumberbatch in a rather stunning way stood when we entered. He spoke in a distinctly American Midwest accent. "I'm Swagley. Thank you for coming to meet with me." His voice was kind, but something about the way he spoke felt like it was peeling back my skin.

"Thank you for agreeing to meet with us," I said and offered my hand.

He shook it and then said, "I understand your desire to be sure the book is in good hands, and I truly appreciate your care." He smiled, and I got the same cold sensation I felt when I met Erika Weber. "But let me be clear—this kind of meeting is extremely rare. I hope you appreciate the privilege you have attained."

Now, I was used to white guys using their privilege, but typically, they were pretty oblivious to that privilege. This guy knew what he had and wasn't afraid to use it, which I respected in a completely terrifying way. "I understand, sir. Thank you again."

He gestured for me to sit in the chair opposite and for my friends to also take seats. I couldn't help but notice his henchmen did not sit. I supposed if they had to spring into action to subdue or even kill us, it was easier to do that from a standing position.

"May I offer you something to drink? They make Coke just like they did at the soda counters when my mother was a child." Before we could accept or decline his offer, he held up four fingers and ordered us each a soda. "Do you want any food? A burger made with all-American beef, perhaps?"

I shook my head. "No, thank you. We just ate," I said as if he didn't already know that. "You have American beef flown in?"

"Oh no," Swagley smiled. "I fly it in myself."

Of course, he does, I thought. "Ah, very good," I said in some sort of throwback British way that was, I suppose, a result of me feeling inferior since I didn't fly in my own meat. I needed to make a mental note to do that soon. Gracious.

The waiter brought us our sodas, and after we each took a

sip under Swagley's gaze and smiled like it was the nectar of the gods, he said, "I would very much like to see the book, please."

Again, his manners were impeccable, and again, I got the distinct impression that they were a cover for far more unpleasant behaviors if I did not comply and quickly. So I reached into my bag, lifted out the fake dictionary, and opened it while keeping the combination as hidden as possible. In retrospect, such an attempt at secrecy seemed silly, but all I can say is that I had read the warning about protecting your PIN on ATMs far too many times.

Once the book was open, I very carefully lifted the book out and set it gently in front of Swagley. On a whim, I had wrapped the book in a purple silk scarf Beattie had bought me on our first day here. I felt like it gave the fake copy a more formal presence and, hopefully, added to the impression that the book was old and tender.

Swagley stared at the cover for a bit and then slowly lifted it to study a few of the pages below it. He then signaled for one of the men nearby to come over. As he walked over, he took what looked like a jeweler's loupe from his front pocket, placed it in his eye socket, and then took the book from his boss.

With gentle care, he examined the entire book: spine, binding, and each individual page. He rubbed one of the pages between his fingers and even sniffed it. After he was done—and I was nearly faint from lack of oxygen since I'd been holding my breath—he gave Swagley a single nod and then stepped back into formation.

"Very good," Swagley said before gesturing for another man to come forward and place a very nice leather briefcase on the table. "Feel free to count it. I will not be offended."

Oddly enough, I thought it very likely that this gangster had a high code of ethics in his own warped way, and I felt confident he had not shortchanged us even a single dollar. I did pop open the case and looked inside as a sort of performance. "We won't need to count it. I'm sure you are true to your word."

Swagley smiled. "As are you, Ms. Baxter. In fact, if you and your colleagues might be interested, I have another business proposition for you."

At this, I saw Adaire flinch, and then he said, "Forgive me, but my agreement with my employer does not allow me to engage in other work without their express permission. So I will excuse myself." He looked at me and then at Swagley. "If that is all right with you."

"Of course. My colleague here will walk you out and suggest a café where you might comfortably wait until we are done with our business." Swagley stood and extended his hand. "It was nice to meet you, Mr. Anderson."

Adaire smiled at me tightly and then followed one of the bodyguards out of the café. I felt my chest tighten just a little at the sight of Adaire leaving, but fortunately, Aaran and Beattie didn't make any move to leave.

"The two of you are willing to hear my offer to Ms. Baxter and to, perhaps, act as her associates?" Swagley said to my two remaining friends.

Both Aaran and Beattie nodded, and so Swagley continued. "Very good. Ms. Baxter, I have two more books of a, shall we say, rare nature that I could use your skills to acquire. Might you be interested?"

This was it, the moment that Inga and Gunnar had hoped might happen. My heart started racing, and I had to take a breath to gather my thoughts and think about how I might respond if this was a normal situation. "Can you tell me a bit more about the books and your proposed arrangement?"

"While I do not want to divulge the details about the books until we have come to an agreement, for obvious reasons, I can tell you that they are both collections of handwritten stories from a similar time period, and they are both here in Reykjavik with private collectors." He studied my face for a minute, and when I nodded, he continued. "By way of our business, I would be willing to pay you ten percent of what I pay for each book with an additional ten percent if the sales are kept completely private."

I studied him for a minute, trying to seem puzzled. I really needed to take some acting classes. "Those terms sound fine, but why do you want the sales private? Are you wanting to avoid the hassles of being approached by other collectors?" I was really playing naive here, but I decided to go with it.

He smiled. "Something like that," he said. "How does this proposition sound to you? Would you like a day or two to think about it?"

I shook my head. "We are leaving in three days, so if you would like my help, I'm happy to provide it. But I will need to work quickly given the short timeline for the rest of my trip."

Swagley smiled, and that same chill passed from my head to my toes. "Excellent. In my business, a handshake is considered binding." He put out his hand, and I gritted my teeth as I shook it. "Very good." He passed a piece of paper across the table to me. "Everything you need to know about the books I wish to acquire is here. You may contact Ms. Weber if you have any questions."

He tilted his head toward the back of the room, where I was not surprised to see Erika Weber. She smiled at me, and I shivered again. I was going to have to wear more layers if I saw these two much more.

"All right. I'll be in touch as soon as I can. Thank you," I said as I stood up.

Swagley rose again and shook each of our hands. "It was nice to meet you all."

. . .

WE PROCEEDED out of the café. I tried to keep my face calm and composed, but inside, my mind was bouncing between excitement that we'd been successful at passing off a forgery and getting ourselves into Swagley's fold—so to speak—and absolute and utter terror for the same reasons.

At the door, one of Swagley's men pointed to a small storefront three doors up and said we could find our friend there. I smiled and thanked the man, and the three of us trudged up the street.

Inside, Adaire was sipping a coffee, or at least pretending to, and when we entered, he didn't even smile. He did take my hand when I sat down next to him, and I could feel his hand shaking. Clearly, I wasn't the only one who was afraid.

I wasn't sure exactly what one did when one had just been recruited as a buyer for a mob boss, but I figured a good place to start was to read the information about the books he gave me. Given that we were still likely being watched, I knew we needed to keep our composure and keep acting our parts, so I turned to Adaire and said, "I'm going to look at the specs of my first assignment. Do you want to know or not?"

Adaire groaned. "I'll know, but I don't want to know the business information, okay? Nothing like that."

I nodded and unfolded the paper. Two neat blocks of text stood out on the white page, one with the title of the book and a brief description and the other with the name of the current owner, owner's number and address, and the maximum price Swagley was willing to pay.

Aaran looked over my shoulder and whistled at the figures, and when I handed the paper to Beattie, her eyes went wide. "Wow, these are high numbers." She squinted. "But I don't know either of these books." She took out her phone and began to tap the screen.

I looked at Adaire. "Are you familiar with them?"

He shook his head. "No, I've never heard of them either.

Maybe they've always been held by private collectors or sold in private transactions?" He shrugged, but something about the way he moved told me there was something he wasn't saying. Now wasn't the time to ask, though.

"Find anything?" I asked Beattie.

She shook her head. "The first one is mentioned here as part of a collection at a small museum in the north of the country, but I don't see a note of the other one at all." She frowned. "That is odd. Even privately held books usually have some records, maybe just in online chats and such, but this one has nothing."

Aaran took out his phone and slid the paper from Swagley in front of him. He tapped at his screen and then turned his phone toward us. "This the first one?" he asked.

I looked at the image of a tiny book being held in someone's hand. It was barely bigger than the size of the person's palm, but it matched the description on Swagley's form. "It looks like it. Where did you find it?"

"The dark web," Aaran said quietly. "Probably means it's being traded in"—he lowered his voice even more—"less than legal channels."

My heart began to speed up again. "Can you find the other one?"

A moment later, Aaran handed me his phone, and sure enough, there was the image of the second book sitting on what looked like a white piece of fabric. Beside it, there was a slip of paper with a figure written on it. "Is this what they're asking for the book?" I said to Aaran.

He nodded. "I think so, yes. This way, they can make a largely anonymous post and still let people know the book is for sale."

I studied Aaran's face for a moment, but he wouldn't meet my eyes. When I glanced over at Beattie, she was studying her boyfriend with a bit of a furrow between her eyebrows. We clearly didn't know everything there was to know about Aaran Anderson.

But I had more pressing things to focus on. "Okay, let's go back to our guesthouse, get refreshed, and I'll put out some feelers." I tried to sound confident, but everything about this situation felt murkier than it had the moment before.

The four of us stood, and Adaire dropped a few bills on the table before we headed out and walked silently to the guesthouse. The place appeared empty, and everything seemed just as it had been when we'd left a few hours before, but I couldn't shake the sense that something was off. I didn't know why, but I did know I needed to trust myself.

So I set up my laptop in my room, connected to the Wi-Fi, and had Aaran give me a quick tutorial on how to work on the dark web. We also set up a fake email account for me with a very generic address. "Now you can reach out, and we trust that Swagley has done his part to vouch for you."

"Vouch for me?" I said as my brain tried to understand what was happening.

"In this space," Aaran said, "you need different kinds of credentials. We'll have to see if he's given them to you."

"If I need his backing to do this work, why doesn't he do it himself?" I asked as I stared at the screen with the first book on it.

Aaran sighed. "Do you really need me to answer that question, Poe?"

There was this place in my brain that was trying to be ignorant and very, very naive, but when I looked at Aaran, that place sighed and gave up. "I suppose not," I said. "What can happen to me if something goes wrong here?"

"You can imagine that for yourself, lass," Aaran said and then went over to sit by Beattie. "It won't be pretty, though."

I shuddered but went ahead and made inquiries about both books using the email and the screenname Aaran and I had created. "BookGal1331" was interested in both items, and she had money to spend.

I made my offers and closed the computer. "Let's go do something," I said as I hopped up and began to pace aimlessly around the room. "I can't just sit here."

"That's an excellent idea," Beattie said. "But first, please, will you check on BB?"

In the excitement of everything else, the fate of my hamster had slipped my mind, which I felt horrible about. "Oh, yes, definitely."

I took out my phone and called Weber. She answered after the first ring. "Please come to the front door. I'll wait," she said before I even got the word *Hello* out.

With a wild wave, I told Beattie to go to the front door, and just a moment later, Beattie was back with a very wiggly BB in her hands.

"We have him," I said into the phone, but I fought my Southern upbringing hard and refused to say thank you.

"Very good. Enjoy your time in the city," she said and hung up, leaving me with no doubt that we were definitely being spied on here in our room. Goose bumps sprung up on my arms again. I was going to have to give these guys names soon.

"How does he look?" I said as I set down my phone and hurried over to get my own hamster snuggles.

"He's fine," Beattie said as she held him out in front of herself and studied his little face. "I think he's fatter."

"How can you tell?" Aaran asked before giving the little guy a quick pet. "Let's go whale watching."

"Yes, let's. Please," I said. Whales are my favorite animals. There's just something so majestic about them, so graceful as they sing and swim and breach. I'd been on whale-watching tours three times in the US, but the chance to see them in another country was too much to pass up. "Where?"

"I called a friend, and he's ready to take us out whenever we'd like," Aaran said.

Beattie and I looked at each other and then at him. "You already made arrangements?" Beattie asked.

"Aye. Did it this morning before we went to breakfast. We can't be in Iceland and only work, now can we?" He winked at Beattie, and she smiled.

"No. No, we cannot," she said. "Meet you downstairs in ten minutes."

The guys left us in our room to change, and a few moments later, we were dressed in warm clothes and ready to hit the water. I was more than curious, now, about Aaran's past, given what he knew and his ability to conjure up a whale-watching cruise out of nowhere. But I didn't sense any danger, and Beattie was clearly excited, given how she kissed him when we met in the foyer. So I was going to do my best to put my questions aside for the day and enjoy some time on the water.

I HAD NEVER BEEN one to enjoy the beach, but I loved the water, especially if I could be out on it. Every chance I got, I drove over to this little town in Maryland called St. Marin's and took a ride on one of the boats that gave tours out of the marina there. I long ago could have given the tour myself, but I couldn't get enough of the wind on my face and the scent of the brackish air. Besides, the town had the best bookstore, so I never missed a chance to visit.

Now, I was practically vibrating with excitement as I saw we were going out on a small fishing boat by ourselves. Aaran had arranged not only a whale-watching expedition but a private one at that. The boat was really rugged and worn, its green paint tinged gray from the sea air. But there were comfortable bench seats up front, and I was glad to avoid the tourist crowds and rush of photographers running from side to side every time a whale was spotted.

The captain of the boat pointed to the benches, said something that sounded like life jackets as he tapped the top of a trunk by his wheelhouse, and then went inside. I liked this trip more and more because of the lack of fuss.

Adaire and I sat on the starboard side of the boat with Beattie and Aaran across from us, and I figured that way, we could spot whales from almost any direction. The engine of the boat started up, and without another word from the captain, we pulled away from the dock and headed out.

As we went further into the water and the temperature dropped, Aaran told us about the area we were in, the Greenland Sea, and the characteristics of this part of the world's oceans. He knew what kind of fish were here and what we might expect of the weather conditions. And as the boat's loud engine motored along, he shouted his knowledge to us across the small boat's deck.

After about fifteen minutes, he suggested we all sit together so he wouldn't have to shout, and Adaire and I moved to his side of the boat, where I looked continuously around so as not to miss any whales.

I soon lost all interest in looking for my favorite animals, though, because as soon as we were close enough, Aaran said, "Now, we can really talk. We weren't followed, and no one can hear us over the engine."

Adaire slapped his knee. "I knew you had this handled."

I looked from my boyfriend to his brother and back. "What do you mean 'handled?'"

Aaran sighed and lowered his voice so it was barely audible over the engine. "I work for MI6," he said.

"You what?" Beattie almost shouted until she saw Aaran staring at her and lowered her voice. "You're a spy?"

"Covert agent," he said with a little smirk. "And yes. Now,

the two of you are only being let into this information because you have gotten involved with Swagley, much to my chagrin. But my superiors are happy to let you take the lead here and have approved that I tell you my real position."

I looked over at Adaire. "You knew?"

"Yes," he said with a blush. "Because I also work for MI6."

"You do?" I said with more than a bit of awe in my voice.

"No, Poe," Adaire said with a laugh. "But I knew Aaran did because he has helped me with a couple of forgery cases over the years."

Beattie was staring at Aaran, hugging BB tightly to her chest in his bag. "I don't know what to say."

"I'm sorry I couldn't tell you the truth before," Aaran said. "It's part of the job, but I'm very glad you know now. Can you forgive me for lying to you?"

"Forgive you? This is amazing. Now, the two people I love most in the world are secret agents. That's so exciting." She leaned over to kiss Aaran but stopped when she saw how deeply he was blushing.

Her face instantly turned a similar shade of red. "I mean, you know, two of my best friends. . ." Her voice trailed off as Aaran leaned over and whispered in her ear. Then her skin tone went even redder, and I looked away, not wanting to intrude on a private moment.

Adaire and I stood up and walked to the front of the boat, each of us scouring the water for whales or anything else to distract us from the wild make-out session that had just commenced behind us. I couldn't help but think that for a man who was a "covert agent," Aaran was awfully willing to make a scene. But then maybe that was the point . . . who blends in better than the person who doesn't?

A few minutes later, our friends joined us at the rail, and Aaran continued telling us what he'd needed this trip to convey.

"We are being surveilled all the time, even here, I expect, but from a distance at least."

"Like someone has one of those parabolic microphones or something?" I said as I thought of all the spy films I'd seen.

Aaran grinned. "In this case, a parabolic mike would be more likely to pick up whale sounds than our voices. I suspect only visual surveillance at this point, perhaps via drone." He looked at me sharply. "Don't look up."

It was good he said it because I was a millisecond from craning my neck as high as I could in the air. "Right," I said.

"After we have this chat," he pointed out at the ocean and smiled as he said, "we must refrain from talking, at all, about my work, except as a fisherman, and we must be very careful how we discuss Swagley and his crew."

Beattie nodded. "But you are keeping the authorities aware of our comings and goings."

Aaran smiled and pointed in a different direction again. "Yes, we are well-protected."

I looked back at the captain in the wheelhouse, and he gave me a two-fingered salute. "One of your colleagues?" I said.

"Yes, but this is his cover, too. He runs fishing charters as far as you know," Aaran said with a look of warning in his eyes. "I cannot stress how important it is that you not blow our cover. Many lives are at stake."

My love of action films made that line sound a bit hokey to me, and I almost laughed. But when I looked at Aaran, he was dead serious, and I quickly swallowed my chuckle. "Got it," I whispered.

At that exact moment, the most massive humpback whale I'd ever seen breached just a couple dozen yards ahead of us on the port side of the boat, and I gasped. Soon, the animal's whole pod was breaching and smacking the surface of the water with their tails. I knew enough about whales to realize they were probably hunting, but I also believed, with my entire heart, that whales had a sort of magical sense of what the creatures near them needed. Right now, we needed a big show of power and energy—at least I did.

The times I'd seen whales in the wild before, and even once when I'd been allowed to watch the trainers practice with Shamu at Sea World, the animals had seemed to meet my gaze. Shamu had splashed my brother and me over and over again until the heat and tension of a hard family vacation subsided.

On another trip, a mother orca and her baby swam beside our boat. I had just ended a long-term relationship, and I was thirty-seven years old. It seemed like I would never find a partner, and it felt too late for me to have a child. So that mother, I truly believe, gifted me a bit of time with her young child to lift my spirits and support me.

And once, when I'd been kayaking in the Pacific Northwest, I'd almost been overturned by a rising humpback. The animal had then submerged, only to arise just on the other side of me. I took that as a reminder that I was not indestructible.

Today, the whales seemed to be reminding us to play, to find joy, to let go just a little and to have fun. So I did. I climbed up on the bench seat beside me—after asking Adaire to hold my waist because I had not forgotten the lesson of that earlier humpback—and I did my best whale song into the air.

As if I were actually making sense to them, the whale pod got closer, and one great creature swam right beside the boat, her huge eye looking up at me. I'm fairly sure she saw my soul at that moment, and I'm pretty certain I got a glimpse of hers.

For the rest of the trip, we saw whales, porpoises, and even a few puffins on the rocky islands. The animals frolicked, and when Aaran came back from the wheelhouse with a couple of bottles of chilled champagne, we did, too. It was a perfect day, and somehow, despite the fact that a spy in our midst meant things were even scarier than I had thought, I felt safer and more comfortable with him watching us.

As we headed back to shore about sunset, Adaire and I snuggled up on the bench close to the wheelhouse so we could get a little break from the wind. As I pressed my face into his neck, I said, "So your brother is a spy?"

"That's a great movie title," he said, resting his chin on top of my head. "And yes. He is. I am sorry I couldn't tell you."

I shook my head. "First, we are just getting to know one another, and we can't know everything about each other all at once."

"Okay, and second?"

"Second, it wasn't your place to tell me that information, and I respect that you didn't."

"Okay, anything else?"

"If you are a spy, you wouldn't be able to tell me, would you?" I was smiling as I asked, but I also had a bit of a pit in my stomach.

"No, I wouldn't, but I am not a spy." He pushed me away from him gently so that I could see his face. "Truly, Poe, I am just a librarian."

"I believe you," I said quietly, but I wasn't sure I believed that he was just a librarian or that he couldn't tell me he was a spy. I leaned back against him and decided it didn't matter, not today, at least.

7

When we got back to the guesthouse after grabbing a pizza for dinner, all of us piled into Beattie's and my room again. This time, I set the laptop on my bed, and my three friends sat around me so they could see my screen. And as soon as I opened my new email account, I found two messages, one about each of the book inquiries I'd sent.

My initial messages had just expressed interest in each book and suggested a place and time we could meet—the café across the street from where we'd met Swagley, at 10 a.m. and 11 a.m., respectively—and offered a cash purchase at that time if the books were to my liking. I would have to work out how to get the cash, but I presumed that Weber could get me anything I needed.

The first email agreed to my terms and said they would meet me at 10 a.m. "I'll be wearing a purple pocket square," the message said. I was relieved to have fifty percent of the plan down.

Unfortunately, the second message wasn't as accommodating. The seller demanded to know more about me—my actual name and the supply of a photograph—as well as a meeting, on their terms, only after they vetted me. I didn't like the sound of that, and apparently, Aaran didn't either.

He uttered a few explicit terms under his breath. Yet the whole time, he kept his face neutral just in case anyone was watching, not just listening, or so I assumed.

"I don't like that at all," Beattie said.

"Me neither," Adaire added. "That doesn't sound safe in the least."

"I'm not telling them my real name, especially since I only know them as BooksAreLife2233. And if they want to see my actual face, they can come to the café tomorrow to meet. I feel like that's reasonable," I said, trying to feel confident even as I heard the wobble in my voice.

"That's more than reasonable," Adaire said. "Swagley wouldn't gain anything from you being in harm's way, and I'm certain, given what he said this morning about the exception he made about seeing us in person, that he wouldn't make this arrangement either."

"That's a good point," Aaran said. "Maybe you should explain the situation to Weber?"

I thought about that for a moment. I decided Aaran was right and picked up my phone. Once again, Weber answered on the first ring. "Give us a few minutes. I expect you will hear from the seller shortly."

I don't know what happened in the next seven minutes, but when my email dinged with a new message, the seller had suddenly become quite amenable to my terms. Just like that, I had two new appointments to buy two books, and I was about to get Swagley that much closer to being arrested.

Another quick call to Weber confirmed that I could pick up the cash for the purchases tomorrow before the first meeting, and she also assured me that there would be "more than adequate" security available for the meetings. "In a quiet way, of course," she said.

I thanked her for that assurance and hung up. A few minutes later, the men headed to their room, and I went into the bathroom to brush my teeth. I ran water over my brush, put toothpaste on, wet it, and moved the brush to my teeth. And froze.

As quickly as hygienically possible, I brushed my teeth and washed my face, then raced out and hauled Beattie into the bathroom to ask her the question that had stopped me cold.

I turned the shower and sink on full blast, said a silent apology to our host for using so much water, and said, "How exactly is all this going to help anyone catch Swagley?"

Beattie sighed. "I have been thinking the same thing all afternoon. Is he using counterfeit money? Is the money marked somehow so that the authorities will know it's dirty? And will they come busting in to get the money before we make the deal? Are they going to confiscate the money we already have?"

"Oh Lord, I hadn't thought about all that yet. Do you think they'll want our money?" I asked as I glanced out the bathroom door to my suitcase that I had chained and padlocked to the leg of the bed with the fireproof book safe and Uncle Fitz's money inside. "Because that's it, isn't it? The only way this is going to get Swagley caught is if there's something about the money that the authorities can use."

"That's what I think, too." She sighed. "That, or—" She stopped talking abruptly.

"Or what?" I said a little too loudly and then repeated it in a whisper. "Or what?"

"Or this is just one more step in the process," she said. Her eyes were as round as an owl's. "Poe, what have we gotten ourselves into?"

I shook my head and swallowed hard, determined not to cry. "I don't know, Beattie, but I think we may be asking the question a little too late."

. . .

I HARDLY SLEPT at all that night, and after breakfast, when we were walking to meet Weber outside Swagley's café before our first meeting, Adaire asked me if I was okay.

"I just didn't sleep that well, is all," I said. "Nervous about today." I couldn't very well tell him that I was anxious not only about today's meetings but also about what was going to be asked of me next, especially when his brother was probably part of the plan to get me deeper into Swagley's organization. "I'll feel better when this is all over." I wasn't lying, not really.

All night, I had tossed and turned as my brain tried to sort through who was really setting the parameters here and who I could really trust. As I drifted in and out of half-sleep, my mind jumped from thinking that I was in good hands with Officer Jonsdottir and Aaran involved to thinking that perhaps Swagley and Weber were, ironically, more trustworthy because they hadn't pretended to be anything other than what they were. By the time I finally decided to just get up, my mind was buzzing like an old fluorescent lightbulb.

Adaire looked at me closely, but he didn't say anything more, and I was grateful. I wanted so badly to trust him, but right now, I didn't know what to do. And I couldn't lose track of what was happening this morning in my confusion. I had to get through these two meetings, and then whatever came next, Beattie and I would handle it.

Weber was waiting for us when we arrived, and without a word, she handed me two briefcases just like the one I had received yesterday. Then she turned and went into the café.

For a second, I just stared after her, and then I headed across the street, where my friends had already secured two tables. The plan was for me to sit at one to wait for each seller. Beattie, Adaire, and Aaran would sit at the next table over and not engage with us unless something looked fishy. Otherwise, they'd just be friends enjoying coffee and pastries.

I so badly wanted to sit down with them and chat, pretend

all this wasn't happening, eat an entire one of those napoleon-like bars, and then do something completely fun. But instead, I sat down alone, ordered a coffee with a lot of cream and sugar, and prepared to wait.

Fortunately, the first seller was right on time. I recognized her immediately because of the purple pocket square tucked into her lovely pin-striped suit jacket. Her hair was jet black and thrown back in a way that looked carefree but had probably taken seven products and a team.

When she looked my way, I raised a hand, and she smiled and joined me, setting her small attaché case on the table between us. "Thank you for meeting me here," I said.

"Of course, Ms. Baxter. Your reputation precedes you." Her accent was Icelandic, and somehow, I found it a little less disturbing that she was from here. That little bit of comfort did not, however, make up for the fact that she knew my name. I didn't like that one bit.

"Thank you, um . . ."

"You can call me Kiki." She smiled and opened the attaché. "I must not dawdle, I'm afraid. I have another appointment shortly. Please, examine the book as you'd like."

Earlier this morning, over breakfast, Beattie and Adaire had coached me on what to look for to be sure the book was authentic. I studied the spine of the book and the binding, estimated the weight of the paper and thought it matched what was appropriate for the time period, and looked closely at the ink to see if it had the brown shade with hints of red that Adaire suggested would have been the natural dye of choice for this era.

All of those things were in order, so I made my first offer, $10,000 below what Swagley had authorized.

Kiki studied my face a moment and then countered at $2,000 higher. Beattie and Adaire had said that what Swagley was offering was more than fair for the book, so I gladly accepted her counter, especially since it was still well below the maximum.

Kiki and I shook on the deal, and I quickly turned, took out the cash I hadn't needed, and then slid the briefcase filled with my first offer plus the $2,000 for her counter across the table.

"It was nice doing business with you, Ms. Baxter." She stood and walked out. The entire exchange had taken less than ten minutes.

After Aaran casually went out to smoke a cigarette on the sidewalk and to be sure Kiki had gone on her way, he came back in and said, "One down. One to go."

I nodded and glanced at Beattie, who was studying her fingernails very carefully. I expected she was as twisted up about this whole situation as I was.

"Do you want something before the next meeting?" Adaire said as the waitress approached. "Maybe just to keep yourself busy."

"Oh, okay, yeah, that's a good idea," I said as I shifted the leftover $8,000 Swagley had given me into the bottom of my bag.

"Can you recommend something sweet?" Adaire asked when the waitress arrived.

"Do you want very sweet or a little sweet?" she replied.

Adaire looked at me, took a deep breath, and said, "Very."

"I know just the thing," she said before taking everyone else's orders for coffee refills and their own pastries.

My fiddling and stalling had run their course, so I said, "That was easier than I thought it would be."

"It does help to have a"—Beattie lowered her voice—"mob boss grease the wheels for you."

"True," I said. "Maybe he should help with all my acquisitions." I had meant it as a joke, but it fell completely flat and landed on the table like a miss-tossed crepe. "I'll be glad when this next meeting is over. What are we doing after?"

"Want to see a volcano?" Adaire said as the waitress brought our order.

She spoke up in response to Adaire, saying, "Oh, the volcano tours are really fun, but they can be crowded. My cousin does private ones. Want his number?" she asked as she handed me a pastry and several extra napkins.

I set down the plate and noticed writing on the napkin beneath it. I slid the pastry aside just a bit and read, "Inga will meet you at two."

"Yes, please. Let's do it, guys. I like the idea of a private tour." I tapped the napkin gently, as if for emphasis, and then slid my plate back over the words.

"All right, let's do it," Aaran said. "If you don't mind giving me his number . . ."

The waitress took a pen out of her apron and wrote the number on the back of our receipt. "His name is Alex. Tell him Ingrid sent you." She smiled, then walked away.

As I watched her go, I wondered if this entire café was staffed with operatives or if it was some innate talent of baristas to be really good at passing notes. They probably never got caught by their teachers in school.

Aaran made the call, and within ten minutes, we were scheduled and provided, via email, with a list of gear. Because the list was pretty extensive, Beattie and Adaire decided to go buy what we needed while I had the next meeting, leaving Aaran there as my backup. I didn't love that because it was really only Beattie I felt like I could trust at the moment. But I couldn't very well say that, nor could she, given the situation.

So with our pastries eaten and coffee drunk, I moved back to my table with my phone and a game that was so mindless I could win levels without thinking. Aaran took out a book from his pocket and read.

At precisely 11 a.m., a man in a dark hat and a very old-fashioned trench coat came into the café. Unlike the other person

I'd met, this guy hadn't provided any identifying information, but given how squirrely he was and the strangeness of his getup, I knew it was my seller from the minute he walked in.

I raised my hand to wave him over, and he scowled at me before stalking over and saying, "Must you be so obvious," in what was a very English accent. "I am not happy about these meeting circumstances."

"As you said, Mr.—"

"No names," he spat. "Let's just get this over with."

I couldn't argue with that, so I said, "Please, may I see the book?"

"Lower your voice," he said in a whisper that carried far more than any normal tone would have. "Yes, you may see it. But first, you must put on gloves."

I resisted the urge to say, "Have you not heard that gloves typically harm old objects more than prevent their damage?" and put on the blue latex gloves he handed me.

Once he was satisfied that I had complied, he took a box out of his briefcase, slid out an object wrapped in blue velvet, and handed it gently to me. "It is fragile, so please be careful."

I nodded and set the book on the table before slowly unwrapping it. What I saw took my breath away, even though I had read the description of the book and knew it was illuminated.

The phrase *illuminated manuscript* was nowhere near adequate for this gorgeous work. The images were so brightly colored they could have been photographs if not for the richness of the tones. The gold outlines of the various figures and letters were exquisite and didn't look like they had faded at all over the centuries, and the text itself was written in a block handwriting that was not only legible but beautiful, too. To say this book was gorgeous was to say that Elton John sort of liked interesting glasses.

I turned each page with absolute awe, and when I finally

looked up, I could see that my appreciation of the book had eased the seller's nerves just a bit. "What can you tell me about the book?"

At the table next to me, I saw Aaran glance up at me. I was going off-script, but I couldn't help myself. I had to know more about this gorgeous work.

"It's something my father found years ago in an old bookshop in London. He had no idea about its actual value, but he loved the images. And when he found someone who could read Latin, he realized it was old folktales, stories about Iceland that had been written by the Irish monks who first visited." The man rubbed his chin. "I grew up looking at these illuminations and making up my own stories to go with them."

He reached over and gently flipped the book open to a page with a lion roaring behind what looked like the letter R. "This one was my favorite. I used to tell my father a story about the brave lion who defended the village from people who wanted to steal their children." The seller shook his head. "I don't know exactly where that story came from, but it gave me great comfort as a child."

"I imagine so," I said. "Who wouldn't want a lion to protect them from all the evil things in the world?" I could completely understand where this man was coming from. I'd grown up with a polar bear formed in the grain of my bedroom door. He was my protector.

The seller looked at me carefully. "My name is Hugo." He sighed. "I'm sorry I was so worried. You seem like a nice young woman. If I may ask, what do you plan to do with the book?"

Suddenly, I felt pretty horrible about my role in all this. I sighed but tried to keep my face neutral since I knew Swagley's people were nearby. "I'm acquiring it for a collector, a man who appreciates and cares for old books like this one."

"That man wouldn't be, by chance, a man with a certain

type of, shall we say, reach, would it?" Hugo leaned in and studied my face. "Is he holding something over you, too?"

I shook my head. "No, sir." I met his gaze and held it, willing him to see what I was trying to convey. "But if you need more time to think about the sale, I understand." I paused for effect. "We could meet back here tomorrow to finalize the decision."

Hugo sat back just slightly as if he suddenly understood, and then he nodded. "I do think that would be best. The book is very special to me, and I need to be absolutely certain I want to sell." He stood up and folded the book carefully back into the velvet wrapper before holding it to his chest once again. "Thank you, Ms."

"Poe," I said. "You can call me Poe."

"Named after one of the greats, are you? Excellent." He put his hat back on, tipped it toward me, and then left the café.

As soon as he was out of sight, Aaran slid into his chair. "What are you doing?" he asked in a breathy whisper. I supposed he didn't think it would bother Swagley if someone seemed to be acting in his interest.

Fortunately, my mind had been quickly thinking as I talked to Hugo, and I had come up with a reasonable explanation for giving Hugo an out. "I am certain Mr. Swagley wants the seller to be sure of their decision so as to avoid, um, messy situations or unreasonable public claims in the future," I said with far more certainty than I felt. "I didn't want this seller to regret his decision and then try to get the book back through means that might draw more attention to my employer than he would like."

Aaran studied me for a second and then smiled. "Wise, lass," he said. "Very wise." He looked down at his phone. "Adaire and Beattie have finished our shopping. They'll meet us at the house so we can all ride together to the tour's starting point."

"Excellent," I said as I gathered my things. "I hope they packed snacks."

IT TURNED out that our barista's cousin was actually a helicopter pilot, and we were going to be beginning our volcano tour with a flight over the crater. When I learned about our means of transport, I realized that this was, once again, our overseers providing an opportunity for us to communicate with each other and with them without being watched. So far, we'd gone by boat, and now air . . . would a train be next? Hovercraft? Dirigible?

As soon as we boarded the helicopter and donned our headphones, Aaran caught Adaire and Beattie up on my interaction with Hugo. When the pilot, Alex, piped in after Aaran's monologue and said that he was relaying our conversations to Inga, Gunnar, and to Officer Jonsdottir as well, I wasn't sure whether to feel more secure or slightly violated. I opted for secure because there wasn't much I could do about the situation anyway.

"But why not buy the book today, Poe?" Beattie asked. "Get it over and done with."

I shook my head. "It was something Hugo said about if I had been threatened as he had."

Adaire sighed. "Swagley threatened him to get him to sell."

"Hugo said Swagley had something over him, so I think it's more like blackmail." I shuddered. "If that's the situation, I wanted to be sure that whoever is running this show we're involved in is going to return the books I'm acquiring to their rightful owner once Swagley is sentenced for his crimes." I looked up at the pilot. "Could you be sure everyone hears that question and gives me an answer?"

Alex nodded.

"It's one thing for me to help catch someone who is a little shifty by acquiring marked money or something—like we were talking about, Beattie—but if people are being threatened or blackmailed, I don't want any part of that." I felt a little nervous being that bold with my position, but it also felt good, too. I had my limits, and the violation of other people's welfare crossed one of mine.

Beattie leaned over and hugged me. "Good for you, Poe," she said.

Aaran turned from the front seat and said, "I admire you for that stand, but it may have put you in more danger."

"More danger than defrauding a crime boss and working as part of a sting operation to catch him?" I raised one eyebrow. "I don't think so."

"You have a point," Adaire said. "But still, let's not take any more risks, okay?" He snaked his hand behind Beattie and squeezed my shoulder.

"I'll do my best," I said. "But no promises."

Our pilot spoke up, "They have every intention of returning the books," he said. "And you have uncovered just what they'd hoped you would—threats and blackmail."

Aaran nodded. "So now you just have to close the deal with Hugo to solidify the case."

Once again, I was left feeling both relieved and full of foreboding. "We'll hope that Hugo comes to sell tomorrow, then."

"Somehow," Beattie said, "I don't think he's going to be given too much choice."

FOR THE REST of the flight, we were mainly silent except to exude awe over the amazing crater below us. It was remarkable, a deep hole in the ground with a pristine lake at the center. I'd seen images of lakes like this before, but this one took my breath when I saw it in person. It felt magical with the steep sides and the reddish vegetation growing amongst swaths of green leaves. Somehow, just seeing it made me feel calmer, maybe because it reminded me that there were forces beyond the control of human beings.

My sense of peace was fleeting, however, when Alex left the crater, flew east, and set down in a field where a single car was waiting with Inga, Gunnar, and Officer Jonsdottir beside it. I was frustrated and disappointed because, once again, my tourism plans were thwarted by this investigation.

Rational me knew that I should be blaming Swagley and his nefarious designs, but right now, three people were keeping me from a rather nice afternoon hiking at a volcanic crater. "Can't we just have one afternoon of peace?" I said as soon as I was far enough away from the helicopter for my words to reach them.

"We understand your frustration, but—" Inga said.

I didn't let her finish. "No, you don't. This is part of your work. This is not part of my work, and anyway, this part of my trip was supposed to be relaxing. Hunting down a mob boss is not relaxing!" I was almost shouting, and when Adaire pulled me close to him, I realized I was near tears.

Officer Jonsdottir stepped forward and put her hand on my arm. "I understand, and we are asking so much of you. Yes. You are doing superbly well, Poe. You really are." There was a softness in her voice that calmed me, and I wondered if she might have children who benefited from her kindness and understanding, too.

"Thank you," I said after I took a deep breath. "You heard my stipulation about returning the books, and you will do that?"

"Yes," she said, "As soon as we are able, we will, and we will let the owners know that their books will be returned as soon as Swagley is in custody."

Gunnar cleared his throat behind her, and she looked

quickly at him and then back to me. "You have my personal word," she said.

I believed her, and the knot in my chest loosened just a bit. "Okay, so why are we here?" I tried to keep my tone neutral, but even I could hear the edge in my voice.

Officer Jonsdottir frowned. "You aren't going to like this, and I'm sorry we have to ask it. But we need your help with securing evidence about Elena's killer."

"What kind of evidence?" Aaran said as he stepped forward. "You can't really be expecting Poe to extract a confession from Swagley."

"No, not from Swagley," Inga said as she moved closer. "From Weber. She killed Elena."

The bluntness of those words left me a little breathless. "She did?"

"Yes, we found a dark hair on the knife, and a partial fingerprint on the handle matches one of Erika's known aliases," Gunnar said. "But before you ask, no, that's not enough. She could claim that the hair and fingerprint were left from her stay there."

I felt a little lightheaded and started to sway. Adaire gripped me tighter. "This is too much," he said.

I put my hand over his, where it rested on my arm. "What do you need me to do?" I didn't know why I said that, really, except that it seemed like this awful situation would never go away if I didn't get the authorities everything they wanted.

"Are you sure, Poe?" Officer Jonsdottir said.

I nodded, even though I wasn't *that* sure. "What do you need me to do?" I asked again.

"When you give Weber the books tomorrow, ask her if she knows what happened to your friend," Inga said. "Push her, but make it seem like you just need closure."

Aaran sighed. "You don't have anything she can use as leverage?"

Inga shook her head. "Nothing that won't tip them off to the fact that she's working with the police. You have to get her to trust you, Ms. Baxter. Find some way to help her feel like your ally."

"So let me get this straight," I said as I leaned even more heavily into Adaire's shoulder. "You want me to be buddy-buddy with a crime boss's hit woman? Am I understanding that correctly?"

Officer Jonsdottir looked away, and I wondered if she had objected to this plan before they came. I hoped so because it was truly ridiculous.

"Is there no other way to get more evidence?" I asked, even though I already knew the answer. They wouldn't be asking me, of all people, to do this if I wasn't their only option.

"I'm afraid not," Inga said, softening just a little. "We will be close by, and this time, you will be wearing a wire. It's completely safe."

I sighed. "Okay, don't lie to me. I'm not an idiot. You cannot make me completely safe in confronting a murderer." I stood out of Adaire's grasp. "I'll do it, but on two conditions that I want in writing. First, you guarantee the return of the books I have and will acquire on Swagley's behalf and that you let those sellers keep the funds from Swagley?" I looked from Inga to Gunnar to Officer Jonsdottir.

When they all nodded, I said, "Two, we are then done with any and all work for whoever it is you are all working for, the president, the Icelandic police, whoever."

This time, all three of them nodded immediately. "I'll have the paperwork drawn up and will get it to you this evening," Inga said.

"And now," I said, "I want you to leave us alone so that we can take our tour." A sudden thought occurred to me. "We are taking a ground tour of that volcano also, right?" I looked at my friends.

"Yes, you are," Officer Jonsdottir said. "I have secured you the best tour guide around." She looked down at her watch. "He should be here any minute."

As if on cue, a black Range Rover pulled up, and a very solidly built man with a blond beard stepped out. "You ready?" he said with a smile.

I didn't hesitate and walked right over. "Poe," I said as I shook the man's hand.

"Ivan," he said. "You look excited."

"You have no idea," I said as I climbed into the back seat. "You have no idea."

8

Our time at the volcano was amazing. We walked down into the crater itself, and I even braved a dip of my toes in the ice-cold water. We got to see the tiny wildflowers blooming on the crater's sides, and we even got to see a gyrfalcon circling overhead.

The hike was intense, and we kept moving for several hours. By the time we climbed back up and into Ivan's truck, we were all panting, sweaty, and completely worn out. It was glorious.

Ivan had told us the history of the volcano on our hike, and he was quite the naturalist. He told us the names, in both English and Icelandic, of the various flora and fauna we encountered. On the ride back to the city, he talked about the villages and communities we drove through.

I was so taken by his casual but richly detailed touring style that I asked him if he booked day trips for private tours. "I do, indeed," he said. "What are you wanting to see?"

"The day after tomorrow, I'd like to hire you for the whole day to take us on a tour of what you think every visitor to Iceland should encounter. Would you be willing?" I needed something to look forward to, and just the idea of this tour had me excited.

"Absolutely. I'll plan to pick you up at 8 a.m. the day after tomorrow." He had a wide grin, and I could almost see his brain planning our adventure.

A few minutes later, Ivan dropped us off at our guesthouse and waved a hearty goodbye.

"I like that guy," Beattie said as we walked inside.

"Me, too," I said. I wanted to say something about our tour, but we were once again in "unsafe" territory, and I didn't dare give away our plans to Swagley and his associates, who seemed to be everywhere. Instead, I said, "I think we deserve a nice dinner. Gentlemen, can you locate somewhere for us to enjoy and let off steam?"

"Consider it done, lass," Aaran said as we parted ways at the top of the stairs and went into our respective rooms.

I was frustrated beyond belief not to be able to talk things over with Beattie, so once I had finished my shower, I left the water running and signaled for her to come into the bathroom. As she showered, I sat on the toilet and spewed out all I was feeling, from my deep anxiety to my slight excitement to the overwhelming desire I had for this to be over.

She listened patiently to me winnowing through my thoughts about things, and when I finished, she said, "You don't have to do any of this, Poe. We can book tickets and leave tonight. The guys will go with us. It can be over."

She'd said something similar to me once before, and it was a good reminder for me to hear her now. I had made a choice to be involved in this situation, and I could make a choice not to be. It was a perspective I'd forgotten all too often in my life, and it was good to recall that, ultimately, I could choose to leave if need be.

Beattie's reminder charged up my spirit, and I suddenly felt more in control—maybe not of the situation itself, and definitely not of Swagley or Weber but of my own involvement. I was choosing this, and if I chose it, I had to have a reason.

While Beattie finished up her shower, I did a little journaling so that I could dig down into why exactly I had agreed to take on the book-buying assignment in the first place and then doubled down with seeking Weber's confession. I was definitely driven by a sense of obligation and a desire to do the right thing. That was certainly there, but I discovered as I wrote that even more, I wanted justice. I wanted people like Hugo not to be taken advantage of, and I didn't want him to have to give up his book. And I wanted Elena's killer caught, not because it could bring her back but because someone who would kill a person as sweet and kind as Elena was certainly capable of killing again.

But when I kept writing and asking myself why, I found there was yet another more personal reason at the heart of why I had agreed to everything I'd taken on in the past few weeks— from the job with my uncle to this work with the Icelandic authorities and even to my newly-forming relationship with Adaire. The truth was that I was finally ready to live life on my own terms.

For years, I had done what I was supposed to do—the education, the jobs, the relationships. None of that had been bad, but all of it had required me to compromise some crucial element of myself, my time, or my ethics. I was done compromising who I was. So taking on this work to capture Swagley and Weber was me seizing my own power and stepping into myself more fully as the woman who could kick ass and take names, almost literally. Okay, not literally at all, but in a sort of nerdy, bookish way.

By the time Beattie came out of the bathroom, I felt like I had just come through a bookworm's version of those training scenes with the punching bags and long jogs, only with paper and pen and a lot less sweat.

In fact, my energy was so high that I almost marched right out the door to dinner without any pants on. Fortunately, Beattie had my back. "Your underwear is really cute, Poe, but I think pants are preferable in restaurants."

I flushed, then slipped on my black dress pants to coordinate with my fuchsia and pink silk shirt. "Now I'm ready," I said.

Beattie tucked her arm into mine. "Yes. Yes, you are," she said and led the way out.

THE GUYS HAD GOTTEN us a reservation at Dill, an amazing restaurant that was just a few blocks away from our guesthouse. As we walked there, Aaran said he'd asked our host for his recommendation, and when the man had said Dill was the best of the best and had received a Michelin star, Aaran had said we'd go there.

Apparently, the restaurant is typically booked months out, but our host knew the owner, so we were on our way to a chef's table dinner at the best restaurant in the city. "I couldn't believe that he could set it up that fast, but I just got a text from the maître d', and he's expecting us in ten minutes," Aaran said.

I looked at him closely. "Did you say Michelin star?"

When Aaran nodded, I began to skip down the sidewalk. I wasn't exactly as chipper as I was acting that I felt, but given my revelation and this dinner gift from the universe, I was feeling pretty darn good. I figured playing a little might just tip the scales of my spirit right over into joy.

I wasn't wrong. When we got to the restaurant and were led past the other diners directly into the kitchen, where a live edge wooden table for four was tucked into one corner, I let go of everything that had been weighing me down and decided to have a great night.

And the night was great. The food was delicious, except for

the pickled shark, which I couldn't bring myself to try because of too many Shark Week shows and the thought that I might be eating a human secondhand. But the lamb was delicious—I was acquiring a taste for it after all—as were the potatoes au gratin. But the dessert, a skyr-based dish with fruit, was the most amazing part of the meal, light and airy and just sweet enough.

Of course, by that time, I'd had four glasses of wine, so it was possible even cardboard would have tasted good by dessert. But I was fairly certain it was incredible. Fairly.

The walk home was fun since all of us were at least a little tipsy, and two of us—I won't name names—were outright drunk. Fortunately, the tipsy ones got the drunk ones back to our rooms, and we all collapsed for the night.

I was too intoxicated to even be grateful that I wasn't thinking about tomorrow, and I slept like a baby, or perhaps not like a baby; from what I hear, babies don't really sleep. I slept like a log. Like a long-dead log.

After I woke, downed three ibuprofen and two Tylenol, and drank two cups of coffee, I felt almost ready to face what the morning was going to bring. Between the very relaxing night, the promise of a custom tour tomorrow, and the newfound confidence I felt in my decision to take this on, I was practically happy.

Okay, not happy, but at least not terrified. On that front, I felt confident, even if I still hated that this had to be done. I didn't mind so much now that I had to be the one to do it.

We had our delicious breakfast at the guesthouse, and then the guys headed off on some sort of errand they would not tell us about. I couldn't decide if they created the mystery to distract us from the morning's events or if they actually had something planned. I found I didn't have the energy or space to care.

And my slight nervousness at not having them there was completely alleviated when Officer Jonsdottir came in and joined us for a cup of coffee around 9:30, using her pretense that this was her usual coffee shop. We talked about the investigation into Elena's murder, which was both appropriate and a good setup to explain why I was about to press Weber for a confession.

When the officer got up, she left her napkin on the table, and I saw two perpendicular arrows on it, each pointing in the direction of a large man sitting at a nearby table—our security detail. Then I noticed a sign that looked like the one on the women's restrooms.

I quickly excused myself to go to the bathroom and found a tiny woman in a police uniform waiting for me. Without a word, she lifted my shirt, attached a tiny microphone to my bra, and then let my shirt fall back down. She pointed to my chest and mouthed, "Speak."

"Goodness, someone needs to replace the paper towels in here," I said.

The woman waited for a second, then nodded before giving me a thumbs-up and pointing toward the door. Apparently, my wire was in place.

JUST BEFORE TEN, Beattie moved to join the officer sitting nearest us, and while he looked a bit surprised to see her there, he put down his paper and engaged her in a conversation immediately, giving them both a perfect cover for when Hugo walked in a couple of moments later.

If anything, he looked more nervous than the day before, and I tried not to think about why exactly that was. Whatever the reason, it wasn't good, I was sure.

Hugo came right over to me and sat down, the blue package tucked, again, under his chin. But this time, he didn't lay it down carefully. He simply handed it to me. "It's yours," he said. "I'm sure."

I had so many things I wanted to say, to ask if he was okay and what had been said to him. But instead, I simply said, "If you are sure, then I am authorized to offer you—"

He didn't even let me finish. "Whatever you are offering is fine." He kept looking around the room and was edging to the rim of his seat, ready to leave.

I made a split-second decision then and quickly put all the money I had, including the $8,000 that Kiki's transaction had not required, into the briefcase and handed it to him. "It's been a pleasure, Hugo," I said and put out my hand to shake it.

He picked up the briefcase, looked at my hand, and then walked away without shaking it. He moved so quickly that he was out the door in a matter of seconds. I felt horrible. He had been terrified, but I couldn't do anything, not without risking my own safety and his. I just hoped the nice pay day would be some relief for him until he found out he could get his book back.

But at that moment, I had to come to terms with what was coming. I had basically pilfered from my boss, a mob boss, who I would have to lie to. Plus, I had to buddy up to a murderer to try to get her to confess to me, which sounded about as likely as her and I becoming friends.

Still, the course had been set, and the only way I was getting off it was to finish it. So I packed up my bag and headed out, Beattie close behind me, to meet Weber. I knew she would already be waiting since my business with Hugo had concluded.

The walk across the street was both far too short and far too long. When I saw Weber waiting, I didn't know whether to walk quicker or slower, so I just tried to keep an even pace. I was as nervous as I had ever been in my life. Given that I had just concluded my responsibilities to Swagley, it occurred to me that it might be suspicious if I was nervous rather than elated. I was about to get a pretty nice payday after all.

Weber greeted us both and then took the satchel from me. "Thank you. Your business is concluded." She reached into the pocket of her coat and pulled out an envelope. "You'll find your full payment—ten percent of each of the transaction's final amounts—here."

"Um, about that," I stammered. "I paid the second seller more than I was authorized, but the total does not exceed—"

Weber put up a hand to stop me. "We are aware, and the situation is fine. The second seller was anxious, and you are a novice. It is not unusual that you wanted to be generous with him. Mr. Swagley found that endearing."

I stared at her for a minute, and then I said, "Thank you. Well, I guess that's it."

"Yes," Weber said and shook my hand and then Beattie's. "We appreciate your good work. Enjoy the rest of your stay in Reykjavik."

She turned to walk into the café behind her but stopped when I said, "I'm sorry, but I do have one more question." I swallowed the softball in my throat and said, "Do you know who killed our first host, Elena?"

Weber turned back and faced me. "Why do you ask me this question?" Her accent had gotten considerably thicker.

"It's bothering me. The police officer this morning said they weren't any closer to finding the murderer, and Elena was so nice." I swallowed again. "I thought maybe, given your employer's connections, you might have heard some news about that."

"I have not, and if I had, er, news, as you say, I would not be inclined to share that news with you, Poe Baxter." Her tone had grown colder, and her accent somehow even thicker. "It is best if you go now."

She started to turn away again, and this time, I grabbed her arm. She looked down at my hand and then up at my face.

"Please remove your hand from my body," she said, and I

suddenly realized she had probably been speaking kindly before.

"Please," I said. "I just need this closure. You must understand. Surely, in your life, there was something, some experience that you just didn't understand. What would you give to have your questions answered?"

For a split second, I thought she was going to soften a bit and, if not confess, at least give me something. But then her mouth drew into a thin line. "Ms. Baxter, it's time for you to leave. Now."

A man inside the café stepped to the window just behind Weber, and I understood the threat the minute I saw it. I had done my best, but now, I had to stop. "All right. Thank you," I said before grabbing Beattie's arm and pulling her down the sidewalk.

"What were you thinking grabbing her like that?" Beattie asked as she yanked her own arm out of mine once we were a few hundred feet away. "We could have been killed right then."

"They wouldn't have done that. Not out in broad daylight that way," I said, trying to convince myself as much as anybody. "At any rate, it's over. We can relax—"

A hand clamped over my mouth, and I was picked up and thrown into what I thought was a black van. A few seconds later, something landed with a loud thud beside me, and I looked over to see Beattie's shocked face just before black hoods dropped over our eyes.

WE HAD BEEN KIDNAPPED.

THE NEXT FEW minutes passed in a blur, and while I tried to pay attention to distinctive sounds—a lesson I'd picked up from most of the kidnappings I'd seen portrayed on television—I couldn't focus well because I was so scared. I had no idea what was happening or why . . . although I had a guess.

I eventually made my way over to where Beattie was seated against the back wall of the van and wrapped my arm around hers as I sat back. "You okay?" I asked.

"Yeah," she said. "You?"

"Yeah, scared but okay."

"Shut up," a man's voice said from the passenger seat. "No talk."

I felt Beattie tense beside me, and I wondered if it was for the same reason I did—the man had an accent, and it wasn't Icelandic. This realization furthered my suspicion that Swagley was involved. After all, he and his associates were the only people we'd dealt with in Iceland besides Adaire and Aaran, who weren't Icelandic.

Because Beattie couldn't see my face, she couldn't anticipate that I was about to say something stupid as I said, "I did what your boss asked. What is this all about?"

The two people in the front seat laughed. "You did, huh? We'll see what he has to say about that."

I felt myself growing angrier, and while I wasn't quite dumb enough to rage out loud, I did fume to myself about how much I'd done for that man already, about how he'd put me in an awkward position, and about how he'd killed my friend Elena. It might have been overstating it a bit to think of Elena as my friend, but she had been a good person and didn't deserve what happened to her.

My rage must have become palpable because Beattie put her hand over mine on her arm and whispered, "Keep your head, Poe. We will have to think our way out of this."

I took a deep breath and tried to slow my thoughts. What did we know? First, the men were working for someone, a man. They had accents that sounded sort of German, maybe Scandinavian, but I wasn't an expert on accents, so that wasn't particularly valuable information. They were driving a van, a black one from what I saw as I was thrown in. They had known we would be at Swagley's café when we were there. They had some reason for kidnapping two American women who were, to most people at least, simply book collectors on a business and pleasure trip to Iceland.

That wasn't much to go on when it came to figuring out how to get ourselves out of here, and I began to panic.

Beattie leaned over toward me and whispered, "The brothers are supposed to meet us about now, I think. They'll know something is wrong and call for help."

"You'd think our backup would have noticed when I screamed on the street?" I said, my bad attitude still reigning strong. But then something occurred to me. "I'm wearing my wire," I whispered.

I felt Beattie sit up a bit straighter. "Right," she whispered.

"No talking," the driver said this time.

"Yes, sir," I answered in my best subservient soldier voice. I had no idea what a subservient soldier sounded like, but I gave it my all. I had nothing better to do.

After a few more minutes, the van pulled off onto what was distinctly a gravel road, a badly maintained gravel road at that. For the sake of whoever was listening, I grunted loudly with every pothole just to help them get a sense of the quality of the road.

Eventually, we stopped, and through the hood, I could see the contrast of the light at the open van door with the dark interior. Then I felt strong hands pull me up and out of the van with barely enough time to get my feet under me.

Hands on my shoulders propelled me forward, and after a few steps, I heard a door open and felt the warmth of an interior space against my face. We were inside, a fact that was confirmed when, a moment later, the hood was lifted from my face, and I blinked my eyes as what was clearly a massive warehouse came into focus.

The men behind us pushed us forward toward a large wooden dining table that was set up in the middle of the room. I felt a bit like I was approaching the banquet hall of a Viking castle, especially when I saw the beer steins and massive proportions of food laid out.

But any tiny hint of hunger instantly disappeared when I recognized Hans, our fellow horseback rider, at the head of the table on one end and his friend from that trip on the other end. "What are you doing here?" I said.

"I've made you a meal, Poe. Beattie. Please, sit down and help yourselves," Hans said as he gestured at the piles of food before us. "Please, I insist." The levity in his voice disappeared on those last two words.

Beattie and I pulled out the folding chairs that looked a bit silly next to the grand table and sat down.

"Eat, eat," Hans said as he picked up a forkful of some sort of salad and slid it into his mouth. At least he wasn't eating a huge turkey leg and banging on the table.

I filled the plate in front of me with vegetables and cheeses, and when I went to pick up the silver stein near my right hand, I found it was already full. I took a sniff. Definitely alcoholic, but not wine or beer.

"It's mead," Hans said. "Our ancestors' favorite drink."

Beside me, Beattie groaned quietly but then covered up her disdain with a bite of food. With her mouth full, a social faux pas my friend never committed, she said, "Thank you for the meal."

"You are most welcome," the other man at the table said. "Please, eat as much or as little as you'd like."

I was definitely on the side of "as little" and picked at my food, only taking a few bites to seem compliant. Belligerence seemed a bad move in this situation, and now that my rage had cooled and been replaced by a deeper sort of fear and a whole lot of questions, I was able to control myself a bit more.

"I imagine you have many questions about why Greg and I have brought you here," Hans said. "I am most happy to answer them."

I looked over at Beattie, who was eating red grapes as if she'd never seen them before. She nodded.

"Why did you kidnap us?" I asked. I figured it was best to go for the obvious since I didn't know how long this Q&A period was going to last.

Hans wiped his hands on his napkin. "Because you are working with the police, and that is simply not acceptable."

All the blood felt like it drained out of my body and onto the floor, but I did my best to keep calm. "What do you mean?" I asked, trying to stay calm. "You mean about the murder of our host?"

"Yes, well, that, but also on something else, I figure, since they were with you all morning, even after Officer Jonsdottir left," the man named Greg said.

"Either that or you, Ms. Beattie, are cheating on your boyfriend?" Hans added.

I gasped. We had made a big mistake when Beattie had moved over to sit with the guard. How had we thought that was a good idea?

A grape went flying across the table as Beattie sputtered. "Excuse me?" she finally said.

"This morning, you and that officer seemed very chummy. Either you are working with him, or you are interested in dating him, which is it?"

I silently begged Beattie to lie, and, bless her heart, she did, even though dishonesty was one of the things she hated most in the world. "What can I say? He was hot, and I've never dated an Icelander before." She shrugged, and for the men in the room, she probably seemed to be playing coy. But I could tell she was barely holding it together.

Before this line of discussion went further, I grabbed hold of it and said, "But why do you care if we work with the police?"

"Now, that, Poe Baxter, is an even better question. We care because we know better than our competitor what their game is, and if they are able to access all of his affairs, then they will have access to our affairs also. That is not acceptable."

I stared at him for a minute and then shoved a bleu-cheese-stuffed olive into my mouth to buy a couple of moments to think. Once I had chewed and even taken a minute to appreciate the delicious snack, I asked my next question. "You are a business competitor of Swagley's, then?"

"That is well said, Poe. I see you have become versed in the euphemisms for our profession," Hans said as he did a true slow clap in my direction.

The urge to roll my eyes was strong, but instead, I asked another question, "So you were interested in the books I acquired for him?"

This time, my question elicited hearty laughter from both men. "No, Ms. Baxter. Not at all. Our purchases are, shall we say, more tradeable in nature. It was, I assure you, only the involvement of the police that led us to be involved at all."

Beattie sat up and raised her hand, and then, as if realizing she wasn't in a fifth-grade classroom, dropped it and said, "But you were following us long before I sat with the handsome officer this morning?"

"Now that is interesting," Greg said. "We actually weren't. Just like you, we had simply booked a horseback riding experience. But when we saw Erika Weber was waiting to meet you afterward, we decided we might need to keep an eye on things."

"And it's good we did," Hans said, "because when we saw your exchange yesterday and then the one today, we learned you were in business for our competitor. That alone was enough to potentially warrant our conversation here, but when we saw your flirtation with the officer of the law, well, it became imperative that we speak."

All the color had faded from Beattie's face, and she had stopped all attempts at looking like she was eating. I, however, felt like I wanted to eat the entire table's worth of food because when I can control nothing, I eat. It wasn't a great habit, but it had served me well enough to help me survive through some tough years. I resisted the urge to grab the entire bowl of olives with blue cheese and begin stuffing them into my mouth.

"So now what?" I said, all hopes of cordiality long faded into my fear. "What do you want from us?"

"Oh, that's quite simple. We want you to come work for us now," Hans said.

I waited a minute to see if he would crack a smile, but his face stayed completely still and somber. "I'm afraid neither of us knows anything about anything other than books." I wasn't lying, either. "Book collecting and literature are all we know. You have told us that you do not trade in that material, so we aren't of any use to you."

Hans looked at Greg, and Greg looked at us. "We overheard some of the figures you and your employer were offering, and well, it turns out we may be interested in the book trade after all."

I sighed. Clearly, it was going to be a long day.

9

After what they called lunch, Hans and Greg escorted us into another section of the warehouse, where they had set up a makeshift living room with couches, ottomans, and even a TV. I had strange hopes that we would be allowed to watch some Icelandic reality television while they plotted their evil schemes, but alas, we were the ones who were forced to do the plotting.

"Ladies, we need you to tell us what books on this list are actually worth the kinds of sums you were offering in the past two days. Which of these books can acquire us such value?" Greg handed us a two-page list of book titles.

Beattie glanced over it and then handed it to me. I scanned the page and then laughed outright. "You want us to tell you, based on a list of book titles, which ones are the most valuable? Are you serious?" All attempts at compliance had gone out the window at this point.

"Is this not enough for you to guide us?" Greg said with a bit of a pouty face.

"No, this is not enough," Beattie said as she tapped the paper on my lap. "Where did you get this list anyway?"

A bit of a blush ran up Greg's cheek. "A 'most valuable books in the world' list."

"On the internet?" Beattie said. "Just on the internet. Wow." I could almost hear her silently saying, "A couple of geniuses, these two," but thankfully, she held her tongue. "Those lists may be accurate for books that are commonly known, but those books are all held in private collections, libraries, or museums already. You need to find books that aren't known to the world yet."

"And how do we do that?" Hans said, sitting down in a club chair across from us.

Beattie's eyebrows almost disappeared into her hairline. "You want me to teach you what it has taken me two decades to learn?"

"Yes," Hans said as he picked up a paper and pen from a small table beside him. "Please begin."

At this, Beattie burst into hysterical laughter and just kept laughing. After a few moments, she was still deep in the throes of her laughing fit, and tears were streaming down her face.

Hans and Greg were looking less and less amused with every passing moment, so I tried to appease them. "Honestly, it's too much information to teach you. I've been doing this work for years, too, and I don't know half of what Beattie does." I took a deep breath and said words I hoped I didn't regret. "It would just be easier if we did it for you."

That stopped Beattie's laughter abruptly as she turned to me and said, "What? We are not helping these people discover rare books to buy."

I tilted my head and looked at her. "Do you think we have a choice? And quite seriously, why not?"

"Because they are gangsters," Beattie said. "That's why."

"Hey, hey," Greg said. "We are not gangsters. Do you see any Tommy guns or fedoras here?"

I rolled my eyes and turned back to Beattie. "Seriously, we

don't have any choice." I silently implored her not to make this more difficult. While these two men had been remarkably decent for kidnappers, I didn't think it would take much for their gentlemanly facades to fade away.

Beattie looked up at the ceiling and tapped her fingernails together. A few moments later, she looked from Hans to Greg and said, "I have two questions before I decide if I will help. First, will you acquire the books with legal tender and offer a fair price?"

Hans and Greg looked at each other, and then both nodded.

"Good, and will you refrain from any coercive techniques to 'encourage'"—she made air quotes—"your sellers to part with their books?"

"Yes," Hans said without even a glance at Greg. "You may be misunderstanding our purpose here, and that is our fault. We are hoping to, let's say, transition our business into something more, well, clean, and it seems that perhaps the book trade is one way for us to do that."

"So you're going to use the sale of the books to launder your money?" I said and thanked *Ozark* and Jason Bateman for my apparently thorough knowledge of money laundering practices.

A smile slowly broke across Hans's face. "You are a smart cookie, Poe Baxter. A smart cookie. But let's leave that question unanswered, shall we?"

I looked over at Beattie, and she shrugged. She'd realized that we were stuck, and our best bet to get out of here was to help these men with their acquisitions. Plus, I hoped she remembered that I was still wearing the wire, so maybe we had just inadvertently begun our second sting operation.

ONE OF THE perks of working for mobsters, I discovered that day, was that they had unlimited resources at their disposal. So within an hour, while Beattie and I watched *Love Island*, Hans and Greg secured not only two laptops and Wi-Fi access for us but also two giant monitors, an array of notebooks and nice pens, and cell phones, closely monitored of course, for us to contact the sellers we located.

It was honestly kind of luxurious. After years of hoarding any notebook with blank pages remaining and protecting my favorite pens with a dragon's fierceness, I had everything I wanted in terms of supplies. A woman could get used to this or could have if she weren't being watched by a very large man every minute.

One of those large men, who said we could call him Frank, had enjoyed booing and cheering with us as we watched TV, and I'd even grown to like him a bit. Maybe because of our mutual preferences in TV viewing, he was assigned to be our guard, so as we set up our workspace on a folding table beneath the clerestory windows in one corner of the warehouse, Frank sat nearby chatting about the show's characters. It was almost nice.

Fortunately, when it came time to work, it turned out that Beattie had been paying attention when Aaran had gotten us onto the dark web earlier in the week, so now she plunged us right in as we searched for the books that met Hans's and Greg's criteria—which was, basically, that they were valuable and were quietly on the market.

Within a couple of hours, we had a list of three options, all with ties to northern Europe, a fact we figured might appeal to our kidnappers, and had begun compiling summaries of value to run by the men.

The first two books were collections of Viking sagas like the one we'd acquired for Inga and Gunnar. Each was handwritten and hand-bound, according to the sellers, and each had roots in Denmark. From what we could see in the photos, the books looked authentic, but of course, the photographs weren't proof. We'd have to see them in person.

The final option was a bit unusual in that it was more modern, from the nineteenth century, but since it was about elves, "the hidden people," as the book called them, it was in my wheelhouse. The seller also purported that the book contained sketches of actual elves that were not contained in any other book. That alone had my interest, and if I found that intriguing, I figured buyers might, too.

After we had gathered as much information as we could and stalled for an additional hour or so by pretending to search further, we told Frank we were ready to present our suggestions to his employers. He looked at us firmly, said, "Stay here," and walked out of the room.

That quick, Beattie was back at the keyboard and typing a message to an email address that felt vaguely familiar. I watched her type for a moment and realized she was writing to the fake email I'd set up for our previous buys. Smart woman.

We ARE FINE. *Hope the wire is working. At warehouse. No idea where except that we came down gravel to get here. Will check this email address when we can. B and P*

SHE HIT SEND JUST as Frank came back in the room, and while he looked at us with a bit of suspicion, he didn't say anything.

A moment later, Hans and Greg came in, pulled up chairs, and sat down. "Hit us," Hans said.

I briefly let myself fantasize about hitting them for real, but then I looked to Beattie to begin our presentation. I was trying to pretend I was just in a meeting with the university administrators—a situation I'd been in a hundred times in my previous job as an English professor—and needed them to agree to let me create this new course. I'd never been turned down for a course suggestion, so it was a fantasy that gave me a bit more confidence than our current conundrum allowed.

Beattie went through the various book options, their pros and cons, and their asking prices. "We suggest that you pursue all three with the ultimate goal of acquiring one of the sagas and the fairy book," she concluded.

I handed Hans our written notes about the books, and he studied them before passing them to Greg. "You two are very thorough and quite professional," Hans said with a nod of approval. "I'm inclined to take your advice. Greg?"

Greg nodded. "You're sure this newer book is worth this price." He tapped on the notes about the fairy book.

Beattie looked at me.

"Yes," I said. "The rare illustrations alone make it valuable, but given the Icelanders' affinity for elves, I expect—if you're trying to sell here, which we'd recommend—that you'd find many potential buyers."

"Okay, then," Greg said. "Let's move forward."

With that, we returned to our work area and set up new email addresses for each of us, as Aaran had taught us, and soon, we were drafting messages to each of the sellers to see if we could set up a meeting.

"Where do we want to meet?" I asked Frank since Hans and Greg had gone back to wherever they hung out.

Frank thought a minute and then gave us the name and address of a café that, since I recognized the street name, I knew was in downtown Reykjavik. A flush of hope spread through me. That put us back where we might be seen. I liked that idea.

Beattie and I suggested meetings at ten and eleven tomorrow, two for her and one for me, at the café Frank recommended, and within minutes, we had three appointments set up for the next morning. While we finalized the meeting details

—telling our sellers that they'd recognize us because we'd have a hamster with us—Frank disappeared for a moment.

Beattie didn't hesitate and opened up my old email. There was a single message in the inbox.

WE HAVE YOU ON SOUND.

THAT'S ALL IT SAID, but it was enough. It meant the wire was working, and I felt another wave of hope.

Quickly, Beattie typed in the information about our meetings the next day, and a reply appeared almost instantly.

WILL BE THERE.

SHE CLOSED THAT WINDOW, and when Frank walked in a couple of minutes later, we were back on the couch with the next episode of *Love Island* cued up.

HAD WE NOT BEEN HOSTAGES, the afternoon and evening might have actually been fun. We binged our show, as we started calling it, all day, and by the end of the day, we were betting with candy about who would recouple and who would stay together.

After a yummy dinner of Thai food that Hans had brought in, the two bosses even got in on the action, although Frank, Beattie, and I had to remind them that we didn't have the financial means to bet with real money, no matter how much fun they thought that sounded.

Sometime after we were well into the second season, I

started to fall asleep, and when Hans noticed, he said, "All right, let me show you to your rooms."

Something about the word *rooms*, as in plural, made me nervous, and when I glanced at Beattie, she gave a subtle shake of her head. She didn't want to be separated, either.

"Um, Hans," I said. "It's very nice of you to offer us our privacy, but if you wouldn't mind, could we share a room? We've been friends for decades. We don't even mind sharing a bed." I smiled in what I hoped was more of a sweet than a terrified way.

Hans paused in his walk toward a metal staircase in the middle of the warehouse and turned to face us. "Ah, girl talk. I see, like a slumber party. Just be easy on the pillows if you fight with them," he said with a smile a bit more lascivious than I preferred.

Beattie grimaced and then lifted the corners of her mouth with what I knew took a lot of force. "Sure thing," she said.

He shook his head in a way that made me want to remind him of the central tenets of feminism and then resumed his walk toward the stairs and up to, what I presumed, was the sleeping level. Sure enough, we passed several rooms set up with beds and night tables, all very comfortable looking except for the lack of windows and the heavy metal doors that locked from the outside.

At the fifth door, Hans stopped and gestured for us to precede him into the room. There, I saw two twin beds, two nightstands, and a small bathroom with a shower behind a half-wall on the right. "Thank you," I said.

"You'll find towels and toiletries on the tables, and there are sleeping clothes hanging in there." He pointed to a small wardrobe in the corner opposite the bathroom. "Let us know if you need anything else."

Then he pulled the door shut, and for a moment, I felt like we might truly get a decent night's rest tonight. That possibility fled when I heard the heavy metal lock drop into place. We were definitely still prisoners.

ALL IN ALL, despite our prisoner status, the room was comfortable. The shower had good pressure and hot water, and the pajamas were quite soft and simple—white cotton pants and a white T-shirt. When I took off my clothes, I carefully tucked the wire into the cuff of my pants and set them on the shelf at the top of the wardrobe. I didn't want to sleep in the tech in case I damaged it, and I hoped this hiding place was adequate. Even if it wasn't, I didn't have much choice.

The beds were divine. The mattresses felt firm but were topped with down, and the comforters were down, too. Just the relief that came from lying down made me realize the exhaustion in my body.

As we prepared to sleep, the temperature in the room dropped, something I appreciated since I couldn't sleep well in a warm room, and within minutes, the air was chilly and my body warm under the comforter. I was still disconcerted by the fact that we couldn't get out in case of, say, a fire, but I was so tired from the stress of the day that I was asleep almost as soon as Beattie turned out the light.

THE NEXT MORNING, I woke to the sound of birds singing and the smell of coffee. It took me a while in the darkness to remember where I was, but when I did, I sat straight up. Where was that bird sound coming from?

Beattie was already awake and said, "They're playing bird sounds through a speaker." She turned on the small light between our beds and pointed at the ceiling. "I can't decide if I like it or find it really creepy."

"I'm going with creepy," I said. "I should only be able to hear birds if I can see birds. That's a new life rule for me."

She chuckled. "You smell that, though, right?"

"Yes, and unless they also have air vents where they pump in morning scents, I hope that means coffee is actually ready." I stood up and stretched, finding that I had slept quite well, considering. No nightmares or anything.

"I hope so. I barely slept," Beattie said as she peeled back her covers and climbed out of bed. "Bad dreams all night."

"Ugh. Want to talk about them?" Sometimes I found that discussing my dreams helped dispel the mental ick that sometimes lingered after a rough night.

She shook her head. "Nah. But let's get that coffee. Coffee might help."

We dressed back into our clothes from the day before, and I carefully placed the wire back on my bra, happy to find it safely in the exact spot I'd left it.

The door to our room had been unlocked, and when we headed downstairs, we found another feast on the dining table and an American breakfast feast at that—bacon, eggs, toast, pancakes, syrup, and berries.

But it was the large carafe steaming with the scent of coffee that drew us first. We poured large mugs full, and I added cream and sugar before sitting down to just inhale the scent and take my first sip. It was perfect. Absolutely perfect.

Then Hans walked in, set down a black wand-like thing that reminded me of the equipment they used at airport security, and then scowled at me. "I wasn't naive enough to believe you had come to trust us, Poe, but I certainly didn't think you'd betray us this majestically." His voice was soft but terse. He was very angry.

I quite legitimately had no idea what he was talking about, so I just stared at him, coffee mug halfway to my face.

When I didn't offer a response, he said, "Stand up."

I did so without thinking, and that's when I felt the wire shift against my chest. My stomach rolled, and I briefly considered tossing my coffee into Hans's face, grabbing Beattie, and making a run for it. Fortunately, I thought better of that and, instead, pretended to lose my grip on my mug and poured coffee, very hot coffee, all down the front of myself.

Beattie reacted, as I knew she would, and grabbed a cloth napkin from the table to clean me up. When she turned to face me, I grabbed the napkin, pretended to mop up my chest, and yanked the wire free from my bra in the same motion. Then I calmly handed my friend the napkin without breaking eye contact and finally turned back to Hans, who was watching from over Beattie's shoulder. I could only hope he hadn't seen what I did, and I said a silent prayer of thanks to the universe that I had put on a rather low-cut top the day before.

Hans stalked toward me with the wand raised, and when he was right in front of me, he raised it above my head and began to scan my body. The tool whined when it went past the earrings on my ear and again when it reached my belt buckle, but between my collarbone and my waist, it made nary a sound.

He looked puzzled. After wanding me again, he said quietly, "I hate to ask this, but I need you to remove your shirt." At least he had the decency to blush at his request.

"Why?" I asked, trying to act like I was still lost about what he was doing.

"Because I need to be sure you are not wearing a wire," he said with just a second's hesitation.

"A wire? Why would I be wearing a wire?" I felt a little frantic because, clearly, he had a reason to know I had indeed been wearing a wire, but short of finding it in our room—which brought along all kinds of creepy possibilities about him being in there while we were sleeping—I wasn't sure how he could know.

"Please, just take off your shirt." He looked away then.

I decided that it was just best to do as he asked so that we could move on, so I stripped off my shirt. "My bra, too?" I said.

He shook his head, his eyes still averted. "That won't be necessary."

Beattie scoffed. "Now you have some decency." She was angry, but I could tell she was mostly scared. She still clutched the napkin in her hand.

Hans turned back to face me, asked me to spin around once, and then said I could put my shirt back on. "I apologize. We received some bad information, apparently."

"Apparently!" I said with frustration that, I hoped, masked my intense relief. "Someone told you I was wearing a wire?"

"Not exactly. Someone told us you were wearing a wire yesterday when you met with Erika Weber." He pulled a long hand down his face. "Again, my apologies. They must have been mistaken."

With some sort of inspired wisdom, I decided to tell the truth, at least part of it. "Oh, I did wear a wire to try to get her to admit that she killed our host Elena, but when that didn't work, I did as I had been instructed and tossed it in a trashcan near the café." I hoped his men hadn't been watching us close enough to know that I hadn't thrown anything away.

The tension in Hans's face eased a bit. "Ah, that makes sense then. So it wasn't inaccurate information, simply incomplete," he mumbled more to himself than to us. Then he looked at me again. "Why did you want to know if Weber killed that woman?"

This question surprised me, and Beattie must have felt the same because I saw her posture straighten in the periphery of my vision. "Because she was our friend, and she didn't deserve to be caught up in our mess." I hoped the truth was effective again this time.

Hans studied my face again for just a second, and then he

stood up straighter as if he had just made a decision. "I see. Well, if it sets your mind at ease, I will tell you that Swagley and his people had nothing to do with that woman's murder. It was an unfortunate consequence of surveillance."

I took in a sharp breath. He had not admitted directly to killing Elena, but he had come pretty close. I hoped the wire was still working and his not-quite confession was enough for his arrest.

"Well, ladies, let's eat," he said in a tone so casual that I did a double take.

Beattie looked at me, and then she sat down, placing the napkin carefully next to her and taking a clean one from the place setting beside her. "Let's eat!" she said with a smile.

10

How I managed to eat four pancakes, three pieces of bacon, a bowl of raspberries, and drink four cups of coffee, I do not know, but when I was done, I was a little proud of myself. Eating in the face of adversity. That had to be a little-praised skill, and I felt as if I had regained control.

But once we'd finished our breakfast, we had to do the work of buying books for our new employers, and I suddenly regretted my appetite. I didn't, however, regret my quick thinking to get rid of the wire. Now, though, my light-pink shirt was stained brown, and I couldn't very well conduct business in a coffee-stained shirt.

"I need to change," I said as we helped clean up breakfast, as much to protect the wire in the napkin that Beattie was guarding ferociously as for any other reason. "I'll just run up and put on the T-shirt I slept in. At least it's clean."

Hans waved a hand in the air. "Don't be silly. We have clothes. What size are you? A fourteen in American sizing?"

I looked at him and nodded. He had pegged it exactly. "Why do you––?" I interrupted myself. "Never mind. Yes, if you have a shirt, I'd appreciate it."

"How does a shirt dress sound? Maybe in black with black leggings? Your shoes will work with that, I think."

I looked down at my red Børn Mary Janes and then back up at Hans. He was right, but his sense of fashion was still a bit uncanny. "Okay, yeah, that sounds fine."

When he left the room, Beattie quickly slid the wire into the pocket of her dress pants and said, "I hope that café has a bathroom. I drank so much coffee." I wondered how much of this was simply one of the challenges of a middle-aged body or if she was signaling our friends—if they were, in fact, still listening after being electronically doused in coffee—that we were about to leave. Maybe it was both.

A moment later, Hans returned with my clothes, and I smiled despite myself. They were lovely and, honestly, perfect for me. The dress was black, but it also had tiny, white owls all over it, and the leggings were warm and thick embossed velvet. I was going to look very stylish and funky. I loved it.

I went into the bathroom at the back of the main floor and changed into my new outfit. When I came out, Beattie smiled, and Hans did his signature slow clap, which was very quickly becoming quite annoying.

We moved to the door, where Greg met us with blindfolds. I groaned quietly. "At least it's not a bag over the head this time," I said.

Greg laughed as he tied the black band over my eyes. "Yes, we prefer slightly more pleasant methods when we can use them. Yesterday, haste was of the utmost importance, as you can imagine."

I rolled my eyes behind the dark cloth and said, "Yes, I suppose haste is important in any kidnapping. It's good that you were using best practices there."

Hans laughed so loudly that it startled me, and I flung my arm out to the side, slapping Beattie in the hip at the same time. I took that chance, though, to grab her hand and hold on tight. I was not about to lose track of her today, not for anything. She had the wire, for one, but most importantly, she was really the only thing keeping me sane. Oh, and I loved her. There was that.

Hand in hand, we walked out into a rainy day, and I shivered. Hans had given us our coats to wear, but this kind of rain cut right through everything. I was not looking forward to riding on the cold van floor again.

To my surprise, though, Hans and Greg guided us into the back seat of a very comfortable car. I wasn't well-versed in car interiors, but I was pretty sure it was leather, extremely soft leather. I tried to relax a bit as we drove.

But unfortunately, I was too keyed up to really wind down, and by the time Greg told us we could take our blindfolds off, my nerves were vibrating like a hummingbird's wings. It took my eyes a minute to adjust, but when they did, I recognized the street we were on just as we passed by our guesthouse and saw Aaran and Adaire on the sidewalk out front, talking.

Beattie and I looked at each other, but neither of us said anything. It didn't matter that we played it cool thought because Hans said a second later, "Oh yes, your gentlemen. I thought you might like to see that they are fine." He cleared his throat. "We have kept an eye on them while you've been with us, and it will please you, I'm sure, to know that they have been very active in their search for you."

It did please me, of course, but not for the reason Hans intimated. I was pleased mostly because the guys, *our* guys, had not let on that they knew anything about our whereabouts. They'd fooled Hans and Greg. That alone was a small triumph.

We drove another couple of blocks, and then Greg pulled the car to the curb. "We're here," he said and stepped out of the vehicle.

"We will wait for you inside," Hans said as he followed him.

Again, I was struck with a strong desire to run, but I knew

better. Just because they weren't escorting us in didn't mean they weren't watching or didn't have other people watching. I squeezed Beattie's hand and stepped out.

THE BARISTAS at this café were good, but I couldn't help missing the clandestine possibilities from our other café, a place I now thought of myself as being a regular. Here, though, the pastries were good, and the coffee was excellent. And I didn't have much choice about locale, so I decided to try—at least a little—to appreciate what I could.

We were about fifteen minutes early, so Beattie and I sat down at adjacent tables with Greg and Hans just a few tables away, acting nonchalant in a very non-nonchalant way. No one would ever know they were our kidnappers. Stalkers . . . people would think they were stalkers because they basically stared at us the whole time.

I did my best to ignore them, as did Beattie, and when our sellers came in and headed straight for us, thanks to our apparently accurate descriptions of ourselves, I put aside the pressure we were under and tried to pretend I was just acquiring a book for Uncle Fitz. It kind of worked, and I felt the first fizzes of excitement about the chance to see a new book.

The book that the young man who came in was selling was precisely what Hans and Greg were looking for. Authentic, old, rare, and almost completely unknown to the larger book-trading market.

I examined the book closely and wondered if Inga and Gunnar would be interested in it for the same reasons they'd bought the first one I'd acquired. It was a beautiful collection of sagas, and while I didn't have the tech they did to test the paper and such, I had no doubt it was the real thing.

The seller was asking a reasonable price, and because I kind of wanted to stick it to our "employers," I didn't even haggle with him. Within fifteen minutes, I had made the purchase with the satchel of cash the men had given me, and the seller had left a happy man. I'd had a lot of questions about where he'd acquired the book, about its provenance, etc., and those questions would have been essential if I were buying the book for my uncle, but in this situation, I figured whatever heat might come down on Hans and Greg was well-deserved.

Beattie's sale looked to be going well, too, and when I saw her hand over her cash payment and take the book, I felt like, maybe, just maybe, we were about to complete our obligation and be on our way and onto the next plane back to the States as fast as possible.

Unfortunately, this situation was one of ever-deepening complications, and as Beattie's seller left the café, Erika Weber passed her in the doorway. Weber did not look happy, and when she stalked over to Hans and Greg and began to speak in lowered tones, all the relief I'd felt a moment before got balled up into tension at the base of my skull again.

Beattie caught my eye and shook her head. "Not good," she mouthed, and I nodded.

So bad, I thought.

Despite my desire to figure out exactly what was going on over on the other side of the café, I had to refocus my attention when a middle-aged man in a beanie and an honest-to-goodness handlebar mustache with curls and all stepped up to my table and said, "Are you, by chance, here about acquiring a collection of fairy tales?"

Between the formalness of his question and his whole look, I wondered if he was doing some sort of cosplay, maybe as a made-up Johnny Depp character. Between his breeches cuffed just below his knees, his flouncy white shirt, and the totally nonutilitarian suspenders he had on, he looked like the way Johnny Depp would play a book collector.

Once I got over my initial intrigue at his appearance—and

let me be clear, I wasn't unhappy with his appearance at all; in fact, I liked the look—I managed to say, "Yes. Yes, I am. Please, have a seat." I was tempted to ask his name, but it would not be wise for him if I had such information just in case Hans and Greg obtained it and tried to reach out again. Although, a quick glance over at their table told me that they were completely occupied in their "conversation" with Weber.

"Very good," the man said as he sat down. "I understand from Adaire and Ivan"—he paused slightly after saying their names—"that you are an excellent book collector." He pulled a book bound in red cloth from his messenger bag and set it on the table in front of me. "I imagine you'd like to take a look."

I was still flustered by the names he had dropped, but I managed to pull the book toward me and begin to look through it while I said, just loudly enough to be heard, "How do you know Ivan?"

"Ah, he has been my tour guide on many occasions. And Adaire is a colleague." He spoke so casually that, especially given their distraction, Hans and Greg would have never thought that this man had just told me that he was working for the authorities.

"Ah, I see," I said as I continued to flip through the pages. "The book is lovely, and as you noted, the illustrations are most impressive."

The man leaned forward and said, "The one on page 288 is of particular interest to me." He quickly flipped over the page to an impressive image of a row of what I took to be fairy houses tucked under a root of a massive tree.

However, it wasn't the image that caught my eye but my name, written on a slip of paper that was folded in half. Carefully, I slid my finger under one end, shielding the motion from the view of Greg and Hans by lifting the left-hand page a bit, and read.

· · ·

Stay calm. Stall. We will be there in just a moment. A

ADAIRE. I felt a wash of relief, but then I heard the rising voices from near the window. I looked at the seller and took a risk, "Erika Weber is here."

The man's face pinched for just a moment but then went back to being placid. "The dark-haired woman?" he asked as he turned to another page in the book and deftly plucked out the note as he did.

I nodded as I followed his lead and pretended to study the pages more. In other circumstances, I would have really liked to not only examine the book but read it. My love of all things folklore was never-ending, but right now, I had far more pressing concerns. "What do we do?"

"You," he said with a nod of his head, "buy this book from me now so I can go inform the team." He slid the book in my direction.

I pretended to give it one last look, and then I nodded. "What's your asking price?" I asked too loudly.

The man gave me a figure, and I readily agreed, almost throwing the money at him and putting the book into my bag hastily. The man rose and walked steadily but quickly out the front door. I turned to Beattie, and she looked very, very puzzled.

I started to tell her what had happened, but I didn't have time because Hans came and grabbed me by the arm. "You're done, correct? We are leaving." He hauled me out of my seat and toward a swinging door in the back that I assumed led to the kitchen.

When I looked over my shoulder, I saw Greg take hold of Beattie's arm and begin to pull her from her seat, but just then, Officer Jonsdottir, the man with the handlebar mustache, and a half-dozen other police officers swarmed in through the front door and grabbed Greg.

Hans glanced back and then picked up our pace, jogging us into the kitchen, around a startled pastry chef, and out a back door into an alley, where he threw me into the back seat of a stopped car and forced an old woman from the front seat. Before I knew it, we were flying down the alley at top speed, and the café with Beattie and everyone else was quickly falling behind. All I could do was watch out the back window and try not to cry.

THE RIDE to the warehouse was quiet, even though Hans was doing his best to make conversation. I wasn't sure if he was nervous himself or trying to keep me calm. Either way, I didn't feel like talking and just closed my eyes and let my head bounce against the window.

When we reached the warehouse, I walked straight in, passed right by Frank, and went to my room. The fact that I was calling it my room wasn't a very good sign, I figured, but at this point, I just needed to be somewhere I felt a little closer to Beattie.

After a long hard cry that miraculously turned into a long, deep nap, I wandered back into the main part of the building and dropped onto the couch. Frank was there, watching WWE with an enviable focus, but when I sat down, he turned off the TV and turned to me. "You okay?"

I looked at him and gave him my best "What a stupid question" look.

He had enough conscience to look a bit chagrined and said, "What would help?"

"Mindless TV. Pick something new." I couldn't bear to watch what Beattie and I had used to cope last night, so *Love Island* was out. But thankfully, Frank's knowledge of reality TV was very impressive, and I was soon distracted by the latest season of *Queer Eye*. Antoni could always get my attention.

After a couple of episodes, Hans came in and said, "They have booked Greg. No bail."

Frank looked sad, and I just ignored the information. It was either that or risk getting myself in deeper by saying something like, "Good. He deserves it."

"I'm sending Stephanie out to talk with him." I figured Hans was filling Frank in on the situation, but Frank didn't seem particularly interested. So maybe Hans was just talking to himself or trying to find a surrogate for Greg. I cared even less than Frank.

"You okay here with her for a bit?" Hans said. "I'm going to get some air."

Frank nodded and turned back to the TV. This man loved his makeover shows.

Hans left, and a moment or two later, I heard a car start up outside. Apparently, he was getting air a bit further away.

As soon as the sound of tires on the road faded, Frank stood up and said, "Do you have anything you need here?"

I looked at him and tried to make sense of what he had just said. "What?"

"Get anything you need. We're leaving." Frank turned the TV up, then walked to the front door and slid a metal pipe between the handle and the wall.

As he walked back toward me, I finally registered what he'd said and grabbed my bag. "Just this," I said. My old clothes were upstairs, but seriously, a blouse and pants were quite satisfactory sacrifices for an escape as far as I was concerned. "You're helping me escape?"

Frank walked quickly toward the back of the warehouse. "Of course. Aaran will kill me if I don't."

I almost yelped with delight. "You know Aaran?"

"Yeah. Best man I know." He opened a small door tucked

under the metal staircase. "Also, the most deadly guy I know, so let's get a move on."

Without any further conversation, we made our way through the door and between a few more warehouses that made me think Minecraft might have been invented in this part of Reykjavik. Finally, we came to the world's tiniest scooter, and Frank, who was just about the size of all of the linebackers on the Washington Commanders combined, sat down. When he tapped the two inches of the seat behind him as if he wanted me to get my hips on there, I almost laughed.

Then I remembered I was escaping from being kidnapped and dropped down, wrapped my arms as far around Frank's waist as I could, and held on. My grip wasn't as tight as it might have been, so when he braked suddenly, I barely held onto him by his armpits as I almost flew over his head.

That alone was terrifying, but when he swore loudly and whipped the bike in the other direction just after I got back into my seat, I was even more frightened. "What's happening?" I shouted into the area where I thought his ear was under his helmet.

He shouted something that sounded like *hands* back at me. "What?" I screamed.

Then he threw his head back, almost knocking me unconscious with his helmet but also conveying the information I needed. I looked behind me and saw Hans barreling toward us in his car. My arms suddenly grew another four inches to reach the whole way around his chest, and I laced my fingers together so hard that I was sure they'd be bruised tomorrow. We were in the midst of a chase, though, and I wasn't about to get tossed off this scooter.

One of the gifts or curses I have as a human being is the ability to find humor in even the most awful situations. So as Frank pushed the scooter to its max, I got the giggles. Just the idea of a high(ish)-speed chase on a scooter was humorous, but when I imagined how we looked, a middle-aged woman with wild curly hair holding on to a huge man for dear life while we zoomed through back alleys on a light blue Vespa, I couldn't control myself. Soon, I wasn't having as much trouble holding on because of the speed—which was fast but not, say, motorcycle fast—as I was from laughing.

Frank must have been able to feel my body shaking because, along one straightaway, he reached down and patted my hand as if to comfort me. He thought I was crying, and that got me laughing even more. This kind man was trying to soothe me while he maneuvered a Vespa through the tiniest streets in Reykjavik. I could not imagine a more absurd situation.

Until we hit the outskirts of town, and Frank really opened her up. Now, we were bustling at a speed that was actually a little harrowing, but my laughter wouldn't quit. And when Frank veered very rapidly to the right to avoid striking an overturned farm truck, I felt my left leg kick up and almost over the seat. Fortunately, my foot contacted the chest of a sheep that had escaped from the truck, and I was pushed back down into my seat.

That was it—I was hysterical then. I had just been saved by a rogue sheep as I fled my kidnapper with a double agent spy slash bodyguard giant on a Vespa in Reykjavik, all because I had taken a new job as a book collector for my ancient uncle who never left his bookstore in Virginia. Tears were streaming down my face, and I was shaking with laughter.

After we were clear of the sheep herd, I glanced back and saw that Hans hadn't been so lucky. While I felt a bit of relief that he was stuck, the fact that he was out of his car and trying to visibly shoo the animals off the road sent me into another fit of laughter. Once again, Frank gave me an affectionate pat, and once again, I laughed harder.

By the time he pulled his scooter into a barn off a dirt road a bit outside of the city, I was exhausted from fear and laughter . .

. and I really had to pee. Normally, I prefer a porcelain seat for such business, but when one has the broadside of a barn, one uses it. Nature calls, after all.

When I came back inside the building, Frank looked at me with concern. "Are you okay?" he asked.

I nodded. I'm sure I looked a mess, what with the high-speed chase, the wind, the laughter, and the subsequent tears. "I am. Thanks for those fine moves."

Frank rolled his eyes. "A scooter isn't my usual choice of getaway vehicles, but it was the best the team could do on short notice."

"The team? There's a team?" I pulled a couple of stray bugs out of my hair and found a seat on a hay bale.

"I'm glad to hear you didn't know. That means maybe only my cover is blown." Frank stretched and then slid a cell phone from his pocket and made a call. "Yes, we're there. Lost him a while back. Were the sheep you?" He smiled and nodded into the phone. "See you in a bit."

"Your team orchestrated the sheepocalypse back there?" I asked. "If so, I need to thank one of those beauties for saving my life." I then told Frank about my near spill and my lucky contact with the animal.

He laughed and laughed. "You will have to tell Aaran that one. That's the best." He leaned back on the stack of hay he'd claimed and closed his eyes. "They'll be here, but they're taking a longer route to avoid having Hans see them. Might as well rest."

I looked at the giant across the barn and marveled. He was snoring, full-on snoring, in less than ten seconds. Adrenaline was going to keep me from resting for sure, but even if I had been able to drift off, that chainsaw sound from my rescuer would have prevented any sleep anyway.

11

A t some point, I'm going to learn to think before I act or speak. I imagine it will be on my deathbed where I weigh, very carefully, my final words so that I die sounding profound instead of one of those people who say something like, "Can emus fly?" before they enter the great beyond.

Apparently, however, my consideration skills were not in play in the barn that day because as soon as I heard a car approaching, I ran out and started waving my arms as if the people coming to get us wouldn't know where to come or couldn't, perhaps, see the giant barn on the barren stretch of field. I was just so excited.

Until I saw the faces in the front seat of the car and realized it was Hans and Greg, who had apparently weaseled his way free even without bail. By that time, they were close enough not only for me to identify them but also to see they were smiling. I had just made a huge mistake.

When I burst back into the barn, Frank was already sitting up. "You went out there." It wasn't a question.

"Sorry." I didn't know what else to say. "What do we do?"

"We get smart." Frank was up and moving toward the back of the barn.

"Right, the hayloft," I said as I headed toward the ladder that was resting near where he stood.

He sighed so loudly that I felt it in my chest. "No. If we get up there, we can't get out." He pointed toward a small door at the back of the barn. "We run and let them think we hid."

"Ah," I said as I followed him to the door just as I heard the car stop in front of the barn. "They're here."

I didn't need to see Frank's face to know he thought I was the queen of obvious, and it was a good thing because his gigantic back was already disappearing through the door. I followed closely behind and then gently shut the door behind me. We were back in the open, and given that the barn wasn't that large and had only housed hay, I figured it wasn't going to take them long to discover we weren't in there.

Frank gestured to a copse of trees just across a wide field, then started to run. Fast.

I am not a terribly out-of-shape person, and I had even run a marathon as a fundraiser back in the day. But I wasn't a fast runner, even in a race. My training had consisted of a run for three minutes and walk for two minutes pace. Now, though, I wasn't going to get that walking break. This was a flat-out sprint.

Fortunately, I had worn shoes with closed backs—my favorite clogs would have been a disaster here—and rubber soles, so I was able to traverse the field pretty quickly. Not as quickly as Frank, who was apparently an Olympic sprinter in his spare time, but still, I gave it my all and ducked into the tree cover in time to turn back and see the back door of the barn open.

"Now what?" I said with a hiss as I ducked behind a tree trunk. "Where do we go?

"Nowhere," he said and looked off in the direction opposite the barn. "The cavalry is here."

For a moment, I looked at him and studied his face. "Are the Dutch famous for their horse-riding soldiers?"

He rolled his eyes. "I thought it might help you stay calm if I used American slang."

"It worked," I said with a laugh. "I'm now thinking about Dutch cowboys."

Frank smiled and then led me to the back of the grove. "Do not step out and flag them down." He chucked me on the shoulder.

I liked this guy, I decided, not just because he had saved me but because, even in this situation, he had a sense of humor. "All right, now, don't rub it in."

"Oh, you won't live this down. Wait until I tell Aaran."

I groaned and then sighed with delight when I saw Beattie leap out of the back of a police car. Adaire was close behind her. But Frank placed a hand on my arm. "Wait."

Officer Jonsdottir jumped out of the car and bolted to Beattie and Adaire, pushing them to the ground just before shots rang out across the landscape. A moment later, I heard return fire from off to my right somewhere and caught a glimpse of two figures running in a crouch across the field. "Aaran and Ivan," I said.

"Yes, now stay down and move," Frank said, practically dragging me to the car and pushing me into the passenger's seat as Officer Jonsdottir got Beattie and Adaire into the back and jumped in the driver's side. "Go!" Frank shouted as he turned back toward the barn and began to run.

The officer didn't have to be told twice. She spun the car around and gunned it across stubs of wheat, kicking up dust and chaff as we hauled it for a few hundred yards until we came to a roadway.

There, she executed a perfect drift turn and sped up the

roadway. Within a few moments, we were back in the city and at the police department. There, Officer Jonsdottir placed us in an interrogation room, promised us coffee and food, and locked us in.

Only then did I hug Beattie, who grasped me so tight my ribs hurt, before pushing me away from herself and saying, "You're okay?"

I nodded and looked from her to Adaire. "I am. Frank kept me completely safe."

Adaire gave me a hug, too. "Feel like talking about it?"

A knock sounded at the door, and a young woman brought in a huge carafe of coffee along with what could only be described as a charcuterie board.

"Let me fortify, and then I need to tell you about a hero sheep," I said.

An hour later, I'd finished telling my story and had eaten a very good portion of sheep's milk cheese, another thing for which I was indebted to the sheep of the world. Butterball and I had taken a bit of a nap in one of the very uncomfortable but apparently adequate chairs, and I was beginning to get restless.

I was fidgety, but Adaire was downright frantic with worry for his brother. He paced the small room at least fifty times, and when I tried to get him to sit and let me rub his shoulders, he literally pushed me away, gently but clearly. "I just need to move," he said.

Beattie took my hand, and we made a small circle with our arms so BB could move, too. Apparently, all the men in the room needed activity. I was completely content to sit for my part. I'd already run and bounced off a sheep for the day. My activity scorecard was full.

After a few moments, the door opened, and Aaran, Ivan, and Frank all came in. Six people in this room would have been tight no matter what, but with these three behemoths in the mix, it felt a bit like a sardine can. It also smelled a bit like a can of sardines, given the amount of sweat we'd all exuded during the day. I was ready to get out of there.

"All okay?" Adaire asked in a far more calm tone than his previous pacing had led me to think him capable of.

"Hans and Greg are in custody, this time without bail," Aaran said. "Adding the charge of murder for Elena's death made everything far more serious. We have you to thank for getting that confession on record."

"Glad to do it," I said. "I do have one question. After Frank and I got away, how did Hans get to his partner so fast?" It wasn't an important detail, but it had been bugging me.

Ivan said, "Apparently, they had one of their guys ready to bring Greg to meet Hans. Their rendezvous point just changed when Hans caught you escaping." He laughed. "I heard there were sheep involved."

I smirked. "Those sheep were there for a lot of us today."

That brought a chuckle around the room, and the gift of laughter did its thing, lifting the tension in the room markedly. The six of us made our way out into the main part of the station, and Officer Jonsdottir gave us a quick rundown on the next steps for our two Dutchmen, including extradition and then trial, she expected, in their actual home country of Denmark. Given that the officer she'd spoken to there reported they were under investigation for several crimes, she assured us they would do significant time for their work.

My concern, however, was more about the victims than the criminals. These folks were probably not the most innocent of individuals, given how they were selling their books, but still, they had been conned. "Will the people we bought books from get their books back?" It was the same concern I'd had about the people Swagley had bought from.

"Yes, they have already been contacted, informed that their

items were purchased by known criminals, and asked if they would like to have their items returned or donated to the government," Jonsdottir said. "They have also been told that they need to return the funds they received unless they want to be indicted as part of the criminal proceedings. We expect both sellers here this afternoon."

"And the books?" I said. I'd left them in the warehouse when Frank and I fled. I wasn't about to admit it, but in this situation, I was most concerned about the books.

"They're safe and sound," Aaran assured me. "We retrieved them along with the rest of the evidence for our case from the warehouse once Frank gave us the coordinates."

"And the sellers are donating the volumes to the government as part of an agreement that we will not press charges if it comes to light that the books were stolen, which is likely," Jonsdottir added.

I nodded. "And if the original owners want them back?"

"Then they will receive them back with compliments from the president," a woman said from behind me.

I turned to see Inga and Gunnar standing there, and out of some sort of instinct, I grabbed Inga and hugged her. She stood stiffly as I did so, but when I pulled back, she was smiling. "I'm really glad to hear that," I said.

"Are you okay?" Gunnar asked. "We've all been quite concerned."

I nodded. "I am. Tired but okay." I was suddenly feeling tiredness in my entire body. "I do think I need to sit down, though."

"If it's okay, can we all go back to the guesthouse?" Beattie asked. "It's comfortable, and maybe Poe can get to sleep early."

Aaran and Jonsdottir exchanged a look, and then the police officer nodded. "I'll ask a patrolman to watch the house just in case."

My heart started to pound. "I thought you had arrested them."

Adaire pulled me into his side as I stood up. "They did, Poe. But it's organized crime. We still have to be careful." He stroked my arm as he held me close. "We are safe, though. We're just being extra cautious."

He led me toward the door, and Beattie walked alongside me. Behind us, I heard Aaran and the others talking, and given their tones were hushed, I figured it was something they didn't want us to overhear. I didn't even try. I was too tired and spent to care.

As we stepped onto the sidewalk, the chilly evening air rejuvenated me a bit, and I felt a bit better. "Can we get some beer to drink when we get back? I want to wind down all the way."

Beattie nodded. "I think I saw a liquor store just up the street here. Let's get something."

Adaire nodded, and as we walked up the street, I was sandwiched between two people who cared about me a great deal. For the first in days, I felt safe.

That was until I saw Erika Weber approaching us from ahead. I clenched Adaire's arm and grabbed Beattie's hand. "Look!" I whispered.

Adaire didn't even pause. He tugged Beattie and me behind him into the first open door beside us, and we found ourselves in what looked like some sort of ritual supply store for pagans and Wiccans. Candles lined the walls, and I saw the tree of life and pentacles everywhere. At any other moment, I would definitely have wanted to browse, but right now, we had some evading to do.

Fortunately, the owner of the store—a woman with a flowing skirt and curls tied up in a beautiful halo around her face—listened when I said, "We're being followed. Can you help?" She didn't hesitate and led us quickly around the counter and into the back room, from where we escaped into the alley through my third back door of the day.

As much as I didn't want to, I knew our safest bet was to go back the block or two to the police station, so we sprinted, still linked together, up the alley and tumbled into the building's rear entrance along with a police officer coming in. He looked a bit startled, but he didn't stop us, even when we bolted past him to find Jonsdottir.

We had just made it to the front of the station when I heard a shout from the street. The officer we'd come in with pushed us to the floor behind a desk, and we hunkered down there while the sounds of fighting took place outside. I had no idea what was going on, but I thought I recognized Aaran's voice among those shouting.

The officer who'd let us in stood beside us, billy club out as if acting as our private guard. I appreciated the gesture, but the guy looked like Doogie Howser's skinny cousin. I wasn't sure what he could do if whatever was happening outside came inside.

I heard someone crash through the front door and ducked lower, hoping that whatever was happening sounded worse than it was. Fortunately for all of us, including the officer who might just have been out of his league, the person who had come in was Frank, and when he saw the young kid ready to fight as he rounded the desk and spotted us, he said, "Good work. Let's get them to safety."

I didn't have to be told twice. If Frank was saying we needed to move, we needed to move. I was even ready for another scooter ride if necessary.

Fortunately, "safety" only involved going further back into the building—this time, into Jonsdottir's office, which had, I noted, two doors so we wouldn't be pinned down. I patted myself on the back for having learned something today. I wasn't, though, quite as quick to give myself credit for needing that tidbit of information several times in a single day. That really felt like the once-in-a-lifetime kind of helpful information.

We settled down onto the floor below the windows of the office and waited. Here, the sounds were more muffled, and I wasn't sure whether to be grateful to be spared close proximity or frustrated because I couldn't know what was happening. I decided to just go with vacillating between both feelings.

"What is going on out there?" I asked Frank, who was looming large in the doorway beside us.

Frank looked down at me. "You really want to know?"

I nodded several times, mostly to keep from shaking my head and declining the knowledge. "Yes, please," I finally said.

"Swagley's people heard you were here. They were waiting for you to come out." Frank's voice was even, but I could see the twitch in his square jaw even from below.

"It was an ambush?" Beattie said. "When is this going to end?"

Frank sighed. "This part will be over soon. Aaran's got the situation under control now, so it'll just be a minute."

I relaxed a little, but then I replayed what Frank had just said. "What do you mean by this part?" I shouted as I looked up at him.

"It's okay, Poe. You're safe." He smiled down at me.

I was beginning to think that people saying I was safe actually meant the opposite, and it wasn't lost on me that the big man had not answered my question.

"Aaran will tell us what's going on," Adaire said confidently.

I saw Frank glance down at my boyfriend when he spoke, and something about that glance made me think Adaire might not have as much reason to be confident as he seemed to think.

Still, for the moment, I did feel safe, and I decided to take advantage of the moment. "I'm so sorry we got separated, Beattie," I said as I laid my head on my friend's shoulder. "Were you okay?"

She nodded and put her head on mine. "Aaran got me away from Greg almost immediately, and the rest of their crew was grabbed at the same moment. I wasn't in any danger, really." She reached her right arm over and squeezed my hand that gripped her elbow. "I was just worried about you."

I pulled her arm in close. "I was really okay. Frank saw to that. But let's not get separated again, okay?"

"Deal," she said, and we sat in silence with our heads resting together for a few moments while the shouts began to subside, and the sounds of voices turned into the voices of people we knew out in the main part of the station.

"Stay here," Frank said when the fighting had stopped. Then he turned to the young officer who had stayed vigilantly nearby to assist. "Keep them here until I tell you."

Little Doogie nodded and took up Frank's post in the door. I could see almost the entire room around his super-thin frame, but he was loyal and disciplined. That had to count for something.

Eventually, Aaran came into the doorway and relieved the officer before helping Beattie to her feet, where he gave her a long hug. "You okay?" he said quietly with his forehead pressed to hers.

She nodded. "What happened?"

"It's a long story. I'll definitely fill you in, but for now, can we go get a beer?" Aaran said.

I sighed. "Can you go get a beer for all of us? I just want to sit down on something soft."

"I'll give you all a lift," Jonsdottir said from the hallway. "You've had enough mishaps today to fill a lifetime."

I smiled gratefully at her and leaned into Adaire as I heaved myself up from the floor; the weariness of earlier exponentially increased. "Thank you. I don't think I can walk any farther today."

While we made our way to the car with Frank as our escort, Adaire called ahead and asked if, by chance, we could move a couple of extra chairs and a television into our room. He didn't give all the details to our host, but apparently, the man already knew something because he agreed readily. I figured my friends had given him a bit of information—maybe even the police had —when Beattie and I had been kidnapped. Perhaps for his protection, perhaps to suss out if he was involved.

Given that he wasn't under arrest and we were going back to stay at his home, I gathered he had been cleared, and I was grateful to hear that I could lie down and still have company when we got there. It was going to be cozy in our small room, but I didn't mind cozy after that huge warehouse and the days I'd just had, as long as at least a few of us could shower.

When we got to the guesthouse, our host was outside with a warm neck pillow ready for me. He slipped it around my neck and then draped the softest shawl around my shoulders before following us up to our room with a carafe of coffee, some of the most American cupcakes I'd ever seen (red, white, and blue forever), and a glass bottle of clear liquid.

He set everything down on a small table in the corner of the room and then pointed to the bottle. "I believe you have something like this in the States. Perhaps you call it moonglow."

Beattie smiled. "Moonshine. Is that Icelandic moonshine?"

Our host nodded. "Brennivin."

Just the thought of the pleasant burn of hard liquor relaxed me a bit. "How do you usually drink it?" I asked, trying to be culturally sensitive and kind despite my growing fatigue.

"I like it cold," he said and held up a shot glass. He poured himself a drink and tossed it back. "You try?"

I nodded. "Is it sweet?"

He shook his head as he handed me a glass.

A quick sniff made me think of the rye bread I'd grown to love so well here, and when I tipped the glass to my mouth, that was what I tasted, too, at least until the alcohol content hit me. I sputtered a bit but got the whole glass down before sitting back against the headboard and letting the warmth sink deep into me.

Within a few minutes, I felt much more relaxed. When Aaran came in with the beer and Adaire poured me another shot of Brennivin, I finally felt my nervous system settle down all the way. Of course, by then, I was also about a half-second away from sleep.

But I really wanted to hear what had happened on the street earlier, so I forced myself to sit up straighter and stay awake while Officer Jonsdottir and Frank said their goodbyes and headed out. Frank was staying nearby just in case, and he assured us Ivan was nearby, too. "You're safe, Poe," he said again. Finally, I believed him.

After everyone else had left, Aaran drained his beer and began to explain what had happened. Apparently, as Aaran had said, Weber and some of Swagley's other people had been waiting for us outside the station. They had hoped to kidnap us, much as Hans and Greg had done, and extract information about their competitors from us.

"So basically," Beattie said, "you're saying we could have become pinballs for the various organized crime outfits working here in Reykjavik?"

Aaran nodded. "Kind of. This is why I really didn't want you all to get involved. Inga and Gunnar didn't really have any right to ask this of you, especially given their lack of knowledge about the situation."

I groaned. "Why didn't you say something?" I was a little drunk and a whole lot exhausted, and apparently, I was also kind of peeved.

"I wanted to. I really did. But I knew if I spoke up, they'd make me leave, and they might have recruited you anyway. I thought at least if I stayed close by, I could probably protect you." He ran his hand through his hair. "Some job of that I did."

"Are you kidding?" Beattie said, pulling his hand into hers. "You did a great job. These people were just really determined." She looked at him carefully. "Were you all aware of Hans and Greg?"

Aaran sighed. "Yes, but not by name or face. We knew a Dutch-based organization had moved into the area, and we knew there was a rivalry with Swagley's organization, but I had no idea Hans was anyone other than someone taking a horse-back ride."

"Apparently, he sort of was," I said and explained how he'd said that was all he and Greg had been doing there. "Weber's presence is what made him suspicious."

"So if we hadn't taken that horse tour—" Adaire started.

"Nope. We're not going there. This was the work of ill-intended, self-interested people. We didn't do anything wrong." I was surprised at the strength of my voice. "We are going to hold them responsible in our hearts, and we're going to let their governments hold them responsible in court." I smiled as I realized I was channeling my inner Perry Mason. My mom would have been proud.

Beattie raised her shot glass—her fourth if I was counting correctly—and said, "Cheers to that."

"That's not exactly how you use *cheers*, but tonight, I'm willing to give you a pass," Aaran said with a wink.

"What else are you willing to give me?" Beattie said with a coy smile.

"Nothing here," I said forcefully. "You two, get a room." I giggled. "I mean, go to your room." I got laughing again. "Just leave."

Aaran and Beattie smiled and stood, quite happy to obey my orders. Adaire sat down on Beattie's bed and said, "Do you mind if I stay?" He blushed. "Just to sleep, I mean. Nothing else."

I patted the side of my bed. "Only if you sleep next to me," I said.

He stripped down and climbed in, and I felt him kiss my cheek as I drifted off to blissful sleep.

12

When I woke up the next day, I was revived enough to enjoy a bit more than a chaste kiss from Adaire, and when we finally stumbled down to breakfast at the last minute, Beattie and Aaran gave us whistles of welcome that made me blush from my toes to my ears.

I cannot whistle worth a hoot, so I could not return the favor. I am, however, quite good with double entendre and employed my skills at breakfast. Their blushes were worth the effort.

Because of all that had happened on our intended tour day with Ivan—our not-so-real tour guide—Inga and Gunnar had worked some magic and gotten our flights changed, free of charge, to the next day. I was grateful for both the chance to rest and for what would be, Aaran promised, an epic tour still hosted by Ivan.

After breakfast, we made a quick stop at Inga and Gunnar's offices to hear an update on the situation with Swagley, Weber, and the books they had acquired. It turned out that Hugo had been more than willing to testify that he had been blackmailed—over late taxes of all things—into selling his most precious possession and was quite happy to have it back.

Kiki, on the other hand, had been happy to take the cash for the book she had happened to discover in her grandmother's possessions, so the state library had another piece for its saga collection.

"We really appreciate your help, Poe and Beattie," Inga said. "Had we known it was going to be so—"

Aaran interrupted her. "No, lass, don't dishonor these women's work with your platitudes. We all knew this could be dicey. Let's not pretend otherwise."

To my surprise, Inga blushed and nodded. "Well, thank you," she said and offered each of us her hand to shake.

"Yes, thank you," Gunnar said, "and please, a token of our government's gratitude." He handed each of us a certified check for $5,000 US.

I started to say what years of being a woman had trained me to say and decline the gift, but Aaran once again stepped in. "You earned this money, Poe. Beattie, you, too. Keep it." His tone was firm.

I didn't really need too much convincing. I had developed an interest in building a book collection of my own, and this cash would be a good way to start raising the capital I needed to grow my collection. "Thank you," I said and shook Gunnar's hand.

Then we headed out into the street, where Ivan sat in a Land Rover with a collection of warm hats and a wide grin on his face. "Are you ready?" he said.

I was fairly certain I was not.

I WAS RIGHT. Ivan's idea of a touring speed through the scenic countryside of Iceland was about the same pace I've seen NASCAR drivers take in turn three. I held on and tried to close my eyes only when absolutely necessary. I saw roughly seventy-five percent of the ride.

And it was a spectacular ride. We saw some of the most amazing waterfalls I'd ever seen, and I got to see my first glacier and marvel that an active volcano was below it. We passed quaint villages and some of the most rugged, uninhabited geography I'd ever seen. And when Ivan insisted on continuing our drive south even though the day was winding down, I didn't object. He promised it would be worth it, and so far, he'd fully delivered on his promise of a great tour.

The ending of the day was, indeed, spectacular as we pulled up along a beach covered in black sand and watched a colony of puffins cuddle into their burrows for the night. The birds were the perfect blend of ridiculous and beautiful, and the sunset was magnificent, with the water and a stone arch in the distance. I could not have imagined a more perfect way to end our time in the country.

I dozed for a lot of the drive back to Reykjavik, and when I woke as we pulled into the city, I found I had drooled on Adaire's shoulder. Since I had a bit of a damp spot on the top of my head, it seemed he had returned the favor, and we both wisely decided not to discuss the matter.

I gave Ivan a huge hug when he dropped us off. "It was so nice to meet you. Thank you for all you did for us." I stepped back and looked up at the huge man. "Maybe we'll meet again."

"Oh, I expect we will," he said with a wink before getting back in his vehicle and driving off.

I watched him drive away for a few moments, but I was too tired to try to figure out what he meant.

Inside, after goodnight kisses and a few more words about our wonderful day, we all retired to our original rooms that night. I can't say what everyone else's motivation for this choice was, but I was exhausted and wanted to enjoy our trip the next day.

Plus, I was still not exactly sure where Adaire and I stood with things. Tonight, I didn't have the energy to have that conversation, and since the guys were taking us to the airport in the morning, I thought maybe we could clarify then.

I had just gotten into my pj's and pulled as much of my hair as I could into a knot on top of my head when Beattie said, "So Poe, your uncle called yesterday while you were gone. He has another trip for us."

I dropped my head back against the pillow. "And we go directly there, right?"

Beattie handed me BB, and as if sensing I needed snuggles, he cuddled right between my ear and collarbone and went to sleep. "Yes, if we want. But he understands we've been through a lot, you especially, and is fine if we want to come home for a while first."

For a few minutes, I just lay there, letting BB's breath tickle my skin. I didn't really have anything in particular to go home to, and my apartment wasn't anything to celebrate since it was just a cookie-cutter new condo like all the others being built in Charlottesville. I was tired but thought maybe we could build in a few days of rest when we got to our next place.

"All right, let's do it," I said.

Beattie sat up and looked over at me. "Don't you want to know where we're going?"

I shrugged. "It doesn't really matter as long as we can relax a bit when we arrive. Maybe prioritize that before we do any buying?"

"I like that plan," she said. "And there's plenty to do where we'll be going. Animals. Beaches. Hikes."

I rolled my eyes. "You're dying to tell me where we're going, aren't you?"

She grinned. "Kind of, but if you want to be surprised, I understand."

"Seriously, after all that . . . just tell me." I was honestly kind of intrigued, but mostly, I just wanted to humor my best friend.

"We're going to Cape Town."

"South Africa? Are you serious?" I had wanted to go to South Africa for decades. The nation's history of apartheid and reconciliation has always intrigued me. "Really?" I asked, hoping she wasn't playing some kind of mean joke brought on by her fatigue.

"Really. Your uncle has a few prospects there, and we also, maybe, have a side job too." She said that last part as she walked into the bathroom, and she stayed in there so long that I fell asleep. I had no doubt that was intentional.

By morning, her cryptic statement had slipped my mind, and in the frantic rush to get everything plus our new purchases into our bags, eat breakfast, and get to the airport for our new flights to Cape Town, it didn't occur to me to ask her what she meant.

I probably should have started putting the pieces together when Adaire and Aaran said they were coming along on the trip and when I saw Ivan, Frank, and the mystery seller with the beanie in the airport, but I was still exhausted and also super excited. So it took until all seven of us were seated together—in first class, no less—on our first leg to Zurich for me to realize something was going on.

"All right, someone explain what's happening," I said after we were all tucked into our pods and equipped with the beverages of our choice. I was having green tea because I hoped I'd sleep at least part of this almost twenty-four-hour flight from the top of the world to the bottom.

Aaran turned from his seat in front of me and said, "If you're agreeable—and you don't have to be agreeable, Poe—your uncle has offered to work with us on some forgery and black-market book cases. He has suggested that you and Beattie might be willing to assist as well, but as I said, the choice is yours. He has not committed you, and you will not get any pressure from the rest of us."

I looked around the cabin and, for the first time, realized we were the only ones in first class. "You bought out the entire section?" I said to no one in particular.

"Be glad they didn't get the whole plane," Frank said almost so quietly I couldn't hear it.

I sighed. "I am, at this point, absolutely sure that I will regret asking this, but who are 'they?'"

Beattie leaned up from the seat in front of me and said, "I was about to ask the same thing." If there hadn't been a good four feet between us, and if I hadn't been quite comfortable in my first fully reclined airplane experience, we might have high-fived. Instead, I just nodded more.

The man with the handlebar mustache said, "It's a bit complicated—"

I interrupted. "Okay, first, who are you? I don't mean to be rude, but seriously, this is all a little much."

Frank leaned over from across the aisle and said, "Poe, Beattie, meet Boone. Our boss."

I looked at Frank and then at Aaran before glancing at Adaire, who looked just as confused as I felt. "Your boss? Are you some sort of handler or something?" I asked Boone.

"Something like that," he said with a small smile. "I say this with the hope that you won't find me terribly patronizing, but the less you know about our organization, the better. Just know that we are the good guys, and we only work with other good guys." Boone adjusted his beanie and sat back in his pod, clearly confident that he had given me all the information I needed. So much for not being patronizing.

"Forgive me, Boone," Beattie said with so much contempt that I wondered if her words might slice the skin of the plane and send us plummeting to the ground. "But your organization just almost got both Poe and me killed. I'm not so willing to take your word for it that you're the good guys. We're going to need a lot more information than that if you want us to help."

Aaran hid a smile behind his hand. I suspected he couldn't talk to his boss like that, but he clearly liked that his girlfriend could and did.

Boone sat forward, and a little bit of his smooth hipster sheen seemed to have gotten tarnished. "Yes, of course," he said. "I run an organization that works with governments to help slow down the foreign trade in forgeries and other black-market goods. Beyond that, it really is dangerous for you to know more, but I can say that in this past situation in which you found yourself, you were working, through my organization, for the Icelandic government. Everything was and always will be completely legal."

Frank nodded and caught my eye. "He's telling the truth. We use our skills to help repatriate stolen artifacts, locate original artworks, and, as you just saw, keep rare items from falling into the wrong hands through the wrong means."

I studied my new friend, and I believed him. When I looked to Aaran for confirmation, he gave me a single nod. I had no reason not to trust these two men, even if Boone was kind of pushing my buttons. And I didn't think my uncle would get involved in anything unless he had vetted it fully.

But I wanted to have one more bit of input before I decided whether or not I'd help Boone and his people do what they did. I looked over at Adaire, and then I laughed. His mouth was hanging open, and he was simply staring at his brother. That was all the confirmation I needed.

"So what you're telling me is that you're government contractors who are basically Indiana Jones in the bodies of a fisherman, a bodybuilder, and a hipster?" I said with as much snark as I could muster, given my fatigue.

Aaran laughed. "Pretty much. Does that mean the two of

you will be playing the role of Dr. Jones?" He looked from me to Beattie.

I smiled at my best friend, saw her wink, and then said, "Yes. Yes, I believe it does, gentlemen. You have a deal." Then I took Butterball out from under Beattie's seat in front of me and said, "No snakes allowed, though, okay?"

Order Poe, Beattie, and Butterball's next adventure, *Butchery And Bindings*, here - https://books2read.com/butcheryandbindings

Happy Reading!

A FREE COZY SET IN SAN FRANCISCO

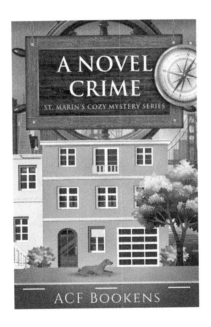

Join my Cozy Up email group for weekly book
recommendations & a FREE copy of *A Novel Crime*, the prequel
to my St. Marin's Cozy Mystery Series.
Sign-up here - https://bookens.andilit.com/CozyUp

ABOUT THE AUTHOR

ACF Bookens lives in the Blue Ridge Mountains of Virginia, where the mountain tops remind her that life is a rugged beauty of a beast worthy of our attention. When she's not writing, she enjoys chasing her son around the house with the full awareness she will never catch him, cross-stitching while she binge-watches police procedurals, and reading everything she can get her hands on. Find her at acfbookens.com.

ALSO BY ACF BOOKENS

St. Marin's Cozy Mystery Series

Publishable By Death

Entitled To Kill

Bound To Execute

Plotted For Murder

Tome To Tomb

Scripted To Slay

Proof Of Death

Epilogue of An Epitaph

Hardcover Homicide

Picture Book Peril - Coming November 2022

Stitches In Crime Series

Crossed By Death

Bobbins and Bodies

Hanged By A Thread

Counted Corpse

Stitch X For Murder

Sewn At The Crime

Blood And Back Stitches

Fatal Floss

Strangled Skein

Aida Time - Coming in January 2023

Poe Baxter Books Series

Fatalities And Folios

Massacre And Margins

Butchery And Bindings - Coming in November 2022

Monograph and Murder - Coming in February 2023

Spines and Slaughter - Coming in April 2023